HER MAJESTY'S CAPTAIN

ELIJAH HER

Cover Design: Elijah Her
Interior Art: Canva
Cover Art: ilywhynot

ISBN: 979-8-9927299-2-4 (paperback)
ISBN: 979-8-9927299-3-1 (ebook)

F90 PRESS

www.f90press.com

For the adventurers, dreamers, and romantics, who believe that love is the greatest treasure, and would brave even the most impossible quests to claim it.

CONTENT NOTES

Her Majesty's Captain includes explicit sexual content. It also touches on themes some may be sensitive to or find triggering:

Detailed depictions of violence and brutality, including death. Graphic depictions of explicit sexual scenes. Struggle with familial and societal pressures regarding gender norms.

PRONUNCIATION GUIDE

Ahrin *(AH-rin)*

Bran *(BRAN)*

Cyanderis *(sigh-AN-der-iss)*

Erius *(EH-ree-us)*

Florwyn *(FLOOR-win)*

Gareth *(GAIR-eth)*

Jasper *(JAS-per)*

Joan *(JONE)*

Malachi *(MAL-uh-kai)*

Maristell *(MAIR-uh-stell)*

Maura *(MOR-uh)*

Naree *(NAH-ree)*

Perpelagust *(PUR-peh-luh-gust)*

Piscia *(PISH-ee-uh)*

Ryung *(ree-YUNG)*

Tae *(TAY)*

Thalassia *(thuh-LASS-ee-uh)*

Zostera *(ZOS-ter-uh)*

PLAYLIST

Just Friends	*– JORDY*
Tidal Wave	*– Chase Atlantic*
more than friends	*– Isabel LaRosa*
Touch	*– Kehlani*
Taste	*– Ari Abdul*
girls girls girls	*– FLETCHER*
Holy	*– King Princess*
Good For You	*– Selena Gomez, A$AP Rocky*
i'm yours	*– Isabel LaRosa*
Obsession	*– Mellina Tey*

Prologue

"Wait," I breathed. "I can still hear them." The brine-laden air clung to me, sharp and overwhelming, mingling with the rancid stench of fish that had long since rotted away in the caravan's timbered belly. The smell permeated the fabric walls, an unwelcome reminder of where we had hidden ourselves. My hand rested on Maura's shoulder, fingers trembling slightly, as we strained to catch the fading voices of the fishermen through the coarse canvas.

We knew their patterns. When they unloaded their catches, when the royal guards of Zostera patrolled the wharves, and most importantly, when the navy's watch grew thin.

"Now," I whispered, my words edged with the thrill of defiance. Adrenaline surged through me as we slipped from the caravan's shadows. The night air met us like a cold slap, a bracing relief against the heat flushing my face. We darted between wagons and crates, past nets and barrels that reeked of salt and seaweed, until the silhouettes of the royal navy ships loomed before us—dark, majestic, and forbidden.

At the base of the gangplank, a lone guard stood vigil. His armor gleamed faintly in the moonlight, the blue sash across his chest bearing the kingdom's insignia: an anchor entwined with coral. He was still, too still, and Maura's whisper came sharp with unease. "Why isn't he moving? It should be the patrol change. Did we miss it?"

Her teeth worried her lower lip as she stared at him, willing him to move with the force of her gaze.

"No..." My voice faltered, thick with uncertainty. "Maybe we're early." My eyes darted over the harbor, scanning the labyrinth of shadows and silvered shapes. Time was slipping through our fingers like seawater, and I knew Joan, my ever-watchful lady-in-waiting, would soon discover my absence.

Desperation drove me as I pried open the lid of a nearby crate. "What are you doing?" Maura whispered, her brows knitting in alarm.

"Just help me," I murmured, the words barely audible over the pounding of my heart. Reluctantly, she pushed the lid aside with me, revealing burlap sacks stuffed with potatoes. I seized one, then another, and hurled them at the guard. The first landed with a splash in the water, the second struck him squarely in the shin.

"Gods above," he cursed, his voice laced with irritation as he drew his sword. He limped forward, peering into the shadows. "Who's there? This is a restricted area by order of the crown!"

Maura and I flattened ourselves against the opposite side of the crate, our bodies pressed into the grainy wood. His footsteps grew louder, closer, until Maura grabbed my hand and shouted, "Run!"

The word burst from her lips like laughter, and before I could argue, she pulled me up the gangplank, our feet light and swift as whispers.

"Stop! Your Highness!" The guard's shout cut through the air like the crack of a whip.

But we didn't stop. We couldn't. Not when the sea waited just beyond the stern.

We ran across the main deck, our boots striking the planks in a staccato rhythm that seemed to echo against the night sky. The ship stretched out before us like a grand cathedral of the sea, its towering masts cutting through the stars. My fingers brushed over the helm as we passed it, the wood worn smooth by hands that had guided this vessel through countless storms and boundless horizons. I wondered how many men had stood there, steering her into the unknown. How many leagues of ocean had she cleaved, how many shores had her shadow graced?

Our sprint slowed as we reached the stern, and Maura leaned over the railing, her face illuminated by moonlight. Her gaze was fixed on the endless expanse of water below, the dark waves shimmering faintly, restless and alive.

"If you close your eyes and listen," she said softly, "it's almost as if we're out at sea."

I joined her, my chest rising and falling as I caught my breath. Closing my eyes, I let the symphony of the ocean envelop me. The rhythmic slap of waves against the hull, the distant cries of gulls, the salt-tinged wind that carried whispers of distant shores—it all felt real, tangible. My lips curved into a smile, bittersweet and fleeting. This moment, stolen from the life we were expected to lead, was the closest we would ever come to freedom. To the sea.

These were the moments we clung to, moments that lived on in the fragile space between dreaming and waking. They were the memories I knew we would never regret, the ones we'd treasure long after the world demanded we abandon our wild hearts.

I opened my eyes to find Maura watching me, her brown curls dancing in the breeze. Her lashes fluttered as she turned, her gaze steady and unwavering. "One day," she said, her voice low but certain, "I'll have a ship like this. And when I do, I'll take you with me."

Her words felt like a lifeline thrown into an unrelenting tide. "Forget Zostera. Forget boring Prince Jasper. Before they marry you off to that oaf, I'll find a way for us to sail these waters together."

Her words, though meant to bring hope, was a reminder of the inevitable. My fate was sealed: an arranged marriage to Prince Jasper of Thalassia. In a few years, I would be sent to his kingdom, even further from the sea, bound to a life that would crush the very soul of me.

"You promise?" I asked, holding out my pinky, knowing full well that this was a vow impossible to keep. And yet, in the face of everything, I wanted to believe it. To believe in a future where we could choose our own destinies.

Her hazel eyes softened as she clasped her finger around mine. "I promise," she said, her voice carrying the kind of fierce determination that made me almost believe her. *Almost.*

"Princess Ahrin. Lady Maura."

The voice shattered the stillness like a thunderclap. We turned to find the guard I had so recently pelted with potatoes. He stood at the head of three more navy men, his face taut with irritation. Behind them was Edwin, the royal steward, his thin frame stiff with disapproval.

"How many times must you be told?" the guard said sharply. "This is no place for children, much less ladies."

"Your Highness, Joan alerted me to your absence." Edwin stepped forward, his voice clipped but tired. "Lady Maura, your father will not be pleased to hear of this either. Such behavior is unbefitting of the daughter of the Naval Guard Captain."

He gestured to one of the men. "Escort Lady Maura home."

The words rang like a final decree. I glanced at Maura as we were led from the ship, the cold weight of inevitability pressing down on me. When we reached the docks, she lingered for a moment, her hazel eyes locking with mine. Her lips moved in silence.

I promise.

And then she was gone, her figure disappearing into the night as I was pulled back to the palace, back to duty, back to the life I was born into but never truly chose.

Chapter One

Keeping Vows Afloat

My fingers skimmed the frill of my gown, the fabric soft yet unyielding, like the very expectations stitched into its seams. White, of course—untouched, unsullied. The bodice hugged me modestly, the delicate embroidery tracing vines and blooms as though to shroud me in the beauty of what this day was supposed to represent. It was fitting for a bride, a symbol of purity, duty, and sacrifice. Yet to me, it felt like a burial shroud, binding me to a life that was no longer mine to shape.

"Don't forget to smile, Your Highness," Lady Joan chimed, her voice far too bright, annoyingly so for the weight in my chest. Her enthusiasm only deepened my despair. She adjusted the veil atop my head, the pins prickling against my scalp as they were pressed into place.

Around the castle, the whispers had grown louder. Servants, nobles, even the maids who normally avoided my gaze—they all spoke of my "blessed union" with Prince Jasper. Some approach me with smiles stretched too wide, offering well-wishes for my future happiness, for children, for a life "worthy of my station." They spoke as though this was my destiny fulfilled, as though my life didn't truly begin until today.

But I knew the truth. This was my end. The moment my freedom slipped away like a ship vanishing over the horizon.

I thought of Maura, her laughter echoing in my mind as if it were yesterday. We were sixteen when she promised to save me from this fate. *"I'll find a way for us to sail these waters together."* she had vowed, her voice brimming with certainty. Yet fate had a cruel sense of irony. I would marry Prince Jasper and be brought to Thalassia, the kingdom farthest from the ocean's edge, to rule beside a man I did not love. And Maura... Maura had been lost before she could see eighteen. She was not here to save me, nor to witness how turning twenty-one had sealed my fate.

"Dear, don't be so gloomy. It is a joyous day," my mother said as she glided into the room, her elegant steps reflected in the mirror before me.

"Perhaps for you," I replied, turning from the glass, the thick folds of my gown heavy in my hands as I faced her.

"Every mother dreams of this moment," she said, her smile soft, though her eyes revealed the steel beneath her gentle demeanor. "You look radiant." Her hands moved to smooth the strands of my dark hair that framed my face, her touch light yet practiced. She lied with grace, as mothers do. I didn't look like me, but I knew what she saw. The resemblance was striking—Grandmother always said I was her image reborn. My mother's dark locks, her gray eyes, though I was taller. That, I inherited from Father.

"Queen Naree, the ceremony will begin shortly. Allow me to escort you to the great hall," came a voice from the doorway. A servant curtsied, but her words faltered as another figure passed behind her. My father stepped into the room, his broad shoulders filling the space with an air of quiet authority. His expression softened as his gaze met mine, and for a fleeting moment, I saw the man behind the king.

"Beautiful," he murmured, cupping my face in his large hands with a tenderness that only his daughter ever got to witness. He pressed a kiss to my forehead, his lips lingering as though to stave off the inevitable. His lower lip trembled slightly, and despite myself, I smiled.

"Don't cry, Father," I said with a small laugh, though my voice wavered. For I knew, if he were to shed a tear it would only cause me to do the same.

"My only daughter," he said, his tone betraying the weight of emotions he rarely revealed. "I knew this day would come, but now that it's here.." He trailed off, his expression returning to the stoic neutrality of a king. Still, his eyes glistened.

"Thalassia isn't so far," I said, parroting Joan's words in an attempt to soothe him. "Only two weeks' travel. Surely you'll find time to visit me on that side of Cyanderis, won't you?"

"Of course," he replied, the words an empty promise. We both knew a king could not abandon his throne for such trivialities. And I would be alone in Thalassia, save for Jasper and Joan.

"King Gareth, Queen Naree, we mustn't delay," the servant urged gently from the doorway.

"Yes, yes," my father said, offering his arm to me. "Shall we?"

I slipped my arm through his as Joan handed me the bouquet. Pink roses and white lilies—symbols of love and devotion. Their fragrance was overwhelming, rich and heady, filling the air between us. My fingers traced the delicate petals, their softness a fragile contrast to the weight I bore.

In Zostera, tradition dictated that the bridal bouquet be saved, dried, and placed in a vase on the couple's bedside table—a symbol of love enduring through time under gentle care. Yet as my fingers absentmindedly plucked at a petal, I wondered if love could truly last. If I could find that love with Jasper.

"You'll ruin them if you keep that up," my father whispered as we walked. I looked down to see a single petal crinkled in my hand, its edges torn.

We paused at the great hall's towering wooden doors, the muffled strains of music slipping through as they briefly opened to admit my brothers and mother. The weight of the moment pressed down on me, heavy and inescapable.

This was the beginning of the end.

Fate, it seemed, was truly a cruel jester, and the change in the orchestra's tune was its mocking laughter that interrupted my thoughts.

My father turned to me, his hand steady as he lowered the veil over my face. The fine lace blurred the world around me, a hazy shroud that both concealed and protected. Part of me welcomed this small mercy, this fleeting moment of separation. Behind the veil, I could gather the fragments of myself, crafting the facade of the blushing, joyous bride they all so desperately wished to see.

When we stepped into the great hall, sunlight poured through towering stained-glass windows, gilding the chamber in hues of gold and soft rose. It was beautiful—undeniably so. Every corner was adorned with ribbons and silken drapes, pink roses and white lilies woven into garlands that draped the pews and pillars. The effect was breathtaking, as though the very air had been painted with magic. And yet, to me, it was all too saccharine, a frilly deluge of pink and white that made my stomach twist.

The pews were crowded with faces, a sea of nobility bedecked in finery, their expressions hovering between awe and satisfaction. Most were strangers—names and titles I could not place. Their smiles were polished, their gazes expectant, all turned toward me as though I were an offering.

At the end of the aisle stood my betrothed, Prince Jasper Windham. His posture was perfect, his hands clasped before him in quiet confidence. He was the youngest Windham prince, and to most, the most fortunate. The gods had shaped him into a man of striking beauty—his light brown hair curled at the edges like spun gold, his sharp jaw softened by the warmth of his smile. Handsome, princely, and yet wholly unremarkable.

We had first met when I was ten, the day our engagement was announced. I had despised him then. Our kingdoms were too different, our lives too distant for us to ever find common ground. He had been stiff, cautious—a boy of quiet decorum, while I was wild, running barefoot along Zostera's rocky shores and dreaming of the sea. As the years passed, he had tried to court me, but speaking with Jasper was like speaking to stone. He was kind, I will give him that, and a patient listener. But his warmth never sparked into fire.

I forced my gaze forward, willing my feet to keep moving down the aisle. My chest tightened with every step, the weight of expectation pressing against me like a vice. As we reached the stone platform at the end, my father's arm slipped away. He turned to me, his calloused hands lifting my veil. His eyes lingered, tracing every feature of my face, as though committing me to memory before surrendering me to another.

Jasper stepped forward, offering his hand with a small bow, his smile soft and genuine. His brown eyes shone with quiet warmth, his golden crown catching the light like a halo. Dressed in white and gold, he was the embodiment of every fairytale prince I'd read about as a child. This moment—this man—should have been a dream. And he was, he just wasn't mine.

Still, I smiled—a pale, hollow imitation of joy—and placed my hand in his. His grip was gentle as he guided me up the dais, his touch steadying me as my knees threatened to buckle. My chest felt constricted, my breaths shallow as if my corset had been laced too tightly.

When I stood beside him, my hand slipped free of his, pressing against the silk-covered bone of my bodice. I couldn't breathe. I couldn't focus. The archbishop's words blurred into a distant hum, the weight of the moment suffocating.

My breath was finally let loose as commotion outside the great hall beamed through the thick wooden doors. It was a discordant symphony of chaos: the clatter of steel, the sharp bark of voices, and then, unmistakably, the crack of a firearm. The archbishop's voice faltered mid-sentence, his words dissolving into the silence that followed as all eyes turned toward the heavy wooden doors.

They burst open with a resounding crash, revealing a figure framed in the blinding light spilling in from the corridor beyond. He was massive, a towering man with broad shoulders that filled the doorway, his silhouette made even more menacing by the indistinct shapes of others crowding behind him. His attire was unmistakable—layers of worn leather, a crimson sash looped at his waist, and a hat tipped at an angle that exuded authority. Pirates.

They stormed into the hall, faces partially obscured by dark fabric that wrapped around their lower jaws, leaving only their sharp eyes visible. The captain—or so I assumed—lifted a gloved hand and flung a handful of glass spheres into the air. They struck the stone floor with a crystalline clink before shattering. Smoke curled upward in tendrils, and within moments, the room filled with a dense, choking haze.

The guests in the pews erupted into motion, a cacophony of gasps and screams. Panic spread like wildfire as nobles scrambled to their feet, their silks and brocades catching on furniture in their haste. I turned toward my father, my chest tight with fear. He was already moving, guiding my mother toward the nearest guards.

His gaze found mine then, sharp and frantic, and he broke into a sprint toward the dais. But he wasn't looking at me—his eyes darted to something behind me. His lips moved, shaping words I couldn't hear over the chaos.

Beside me, Jasper was being pulled away by the Thalassarian guards, his normally composed features contorted in worry as he fought against their grip. He thrashed, his golden crown slipping askew, shouting something that sounded like my name. His gaze, too, was fixed on something behind me.

I felt it then—the cold, unmistakable press of metal against the back of my head. Every muscle in my body went rigid, and my breath caught in my throat. My father froze mid-stride, his hands lifting in a gesture of surrender. His face, pale and drawn, was etched with a terror I had never seen before.

Then a damp cloth was pressed firmly over my mouth and nose. A sickly sweet scent invaded my senses, sharp and overpowering. My bouquet slipped from my grasp as I struggled, my hands grasping at the air, but the fight drained from my limbs as quickly as it had surged. My vision blurred, the vibrant colors of the great hall smearing into one another, the smoke turning the scene into a surreal nightmare. The last thing I saw was my father's face, his mouth moving in silent desperation before the world tilted and darkness claimed me.

I awoke to darkness, my head spinning and my arms aching. Panic rose like a tide within me as I realized my hands were bound tightly behind my back, the coarse rope biting into my skin. A rough cloth covered my head, smothering my vision, leaving me adrift in a sea of shadows and uncertainty.

I felt the sway of movement beneath me—not my own but something larger, rhythmic. My body lay draped across a broad surface, hard but warm, the unmistakable solidity of flesh and bone beneath me. A large hand braced my back, steady and unyielding. I was being carried, hauled like a sack of grain slung over someone's shoulder. My heart pounded against my ribcage, frantic as a bird trapped in a snare.

I forced my breath to slow, to quiet the panic threatening to undo me. If my captor knew I was awake, I might lose what little advantage I had. Instead, I tuned my focus to my surroundings, straining to hear, to make sense of where I was.

The air carried the briny tang of salt and the faint cry of gulls. The rhythmic crash of waves reached my ears, mingled with the hollow resonance of boots striking wood—pier boards, or perhaps the deck of a ship. A low hum of voices stirred ahead, growing louder as we approached. The fragments of hurried conversations reached me: warnings of time running thin, of the need to escape before the crown's navy spotted them.

My captor's pace was deliberate, purposeful. Each step reverberated with intent. Then, a pause. A door creaked open on rusty hinges, and I was unceremoniously thrown down onto a surface that yielded slightly beneath me. My breath left me in a gasp, and the sharp intake betrayed my wakefulness. The hood was yanked from my head, and light stabbed at my eyes, forcing me to blink against the brightness spilling in through the open door and small portholes.

"Did you have a nice nap, princess?" The voice was deep, edged with amusement, its tone entirely too casual for someone who had just stolen me from my wedding.

I squinted, the figure before me sharpening into focus. He loomed at the foot of the bed—a hulking man with broad shoulders, his dark coat adorned with gold buttons and a red sash. A tricorn captain's hat perched atop his head, a large black feather sweeping out of it.

"Who are you?" I demanded, my voice low but steady as I pushed myself upright, my movements deliberate despite the ache in my bound wrists. I pressed my back against the headboard, forcing my gaze to meet his, though my heart hammered against my ribs.

His lips curved into a wolfish grin, a glint of teeth behind his dark beard. He turned, striding toward the wooden desk that occupied the corner of the cabin. "If it's gold you're after," I continued, my voice gaining strength, "sullying a princess will only diminish her value. Let me go, and you may yet profit from this madness."

He chuckled—a sound low and rich, mocking yet oddly pleasant. "Is that what they tell you in your marble towers? Fairy tales of pirates lusting after royal maidens, only to ransom them off to the highest bidder?" He placed the hood onto the desk.

And then I saw it.

My breath hitched as my gaze snagged on the tattoo coiling around his hand—a tentacle encircling a trident, with a skull impaled on its central prong. Recognition surged through me, sharp and cold as a dagger. I pressed myself further into the headboard, my body instinctively shrinking away from the man who now loomed like a shadow over my fate. This wasn't just a pirate—it was Captain Erius, the dread sovereign of the Perpelagust Sea.

The sea had no kings, no crowned rulers, no laws—but if it did, he would be its monarch, and his crew the fist that enforced his dominion.

They were a legend whispered in port taverns and screamed in coastal villages. No ship was too large or too insignificant for their plunder—naval fleets, merchant vessels, even other pirate brigades fell to their onslaught. And the land wasn't spared either; villages that dared to prosper along the shorelines were razed without warning, their treasures seized, their people left to the mercy of the tide.

It was Erius and his crew who had attacked Maura's village. Her father, the Captain of Zostera's Naval Guard who might have defended her, was away. When the navy arrived to retaliate, it was already too late. Maura was gone. Erius didn't take prisoners; they took gold, weapons, lives—but never mercy. They killed her.

The weight of memory and fear pressed on my chest, threatening to choke me.

"The colors drained from your face, lass," he drawled, his voice low and laced with mockery. He tilted his head, the feather in his tricorn brushing against his broad shoulder. "Have you finally figured out whose ship you're on?"

"Bran, you're scaring the poor woman."

The voice came from the doorway, warm with amusement but cutting through the tension like the sharpest blade. A woman leaned against the frame, her features half-concealed by a veil of black fabric, though the glimmer in her hazel eyes betrayed her humor. Her attire mirrored the captain's—an indigo overcoat and a red sash cinched around her waist—but the weapons she bore made her station unmistakable. A curved sword hung at her hip, its hilt worn but well-kept, and a dagger strapped to her thigh.

"Apologies, Your Majesty," she said, stepping forward with a languid grace, her slender fingers reaching for the tricorn atop Bran's head. She plucked it off and perched it on her own with an ease that spoke of long familiarity. "My first mate has a penchant for dramatics. Go, Bran, and see that all is ready to sail. We've lingered too long already."

Bran inclined his head, his hulking form retreating as he murmured, "Yes, Captain." The door shut behind him with a heavy thud.

"Y-you're Captain Erius?" I stammered, my voice unsteady as my thoughts scrambled to reconcile the infamous name with the woman before me.

"Not what you expected?" she asked, arching a brow.

"It's just... you're a woman," I said, the words slipping out before I could temper them. They sounded judgmental even to my own ears.

"The sea doesn't care if you're man, woman, or something in between," she replied, utterly unbothered. She unsheathed her sword with a practiced flick and laid it on the desk. "I assure you, Princess, I can be just as terrifying as Bran. Perhaps more so."

I swallowed hard, her words settling like cold steel against my skin.

"Why am I here?" I demanded, my voice firming despite the rawness of my wrists against the bindings as I began to urgently twist in them. "If you think this will earn you the royal treasury, you're sorely mistaken. My father won't barter with pirates. And even if he did, he would only use the exchange to buy time for the navy to hunt you down. There's no treasure to be gained from this."

She tilted her head, smugness in her eyes. "I think you're mistaken," she said, taking a deliberate step closer. Her boots creaked against the floorboards, a sound that seemed impossibly loud in the charged silence. "I already have the greatest treasure in all of Zostera sitting on my bed."

"I am a person, not treasure!" I snapped, my voice trembling with frustration.

She sat on the edge of the bed, her posture as casual as if we were discussing the weather. Her hands resting against the mattress behind her, her gaze drifting lazily to the ceiling. "Tell that to the prince you were being given to," she quipped, the words cutting deeper than any blade.

Heat rose to my cheeks, and I clenched my fists, my movements behind my back growing more desperate. "That prince," I spat, "is my fiancé, and I am not a gift. I am his partner. You stole me away."

"In my defense," she said with a soft laugh, "you looked like you wanted to be stolen."

Her words sent a jolt through me, my fury flaring hot. With a final twist, my hand slipped free from the bindings. The raw sting of the rope against my skin was nothing compared to the fire burning in my chest. In one swift motion, I lunged, my fingers curling around the dagger strapped to her thigh.

She barely had time to react as I pushed her down, the puff of my wedding gown billowing around us like a stormcloud. My knees pinned her in place, my breath ragged as I brandished the blade, its sharp edge poised above her.

She blinked up at me, momentarily stunned, then shook her head with a wry chuckle, trying to push the heavy fabric of my dress out of her face. I adjusted, pulling the fabric back just enough for our gazes to lock fully.

"Tell me why you kidnapped me," I demanded, the dagger trembling in my grip. My voice was low, dangerous, but my heart thundered wildly beneath my ribs.

"You wound me, Ahrin," she said, her tone rich with teasing, though her hands moved underneath my dress to grip my thighs with a firm, unyielding strength. "Do you really not know why I'm here?"

Her words sent a shiver down my spine, the familiarity in her voice pulling at the edges of my memory. I leaned forward, the blade trembling between us, and yanked the mask down from her face. The realization struck like lightning. "Maura?" I whispered, the name escaping my lips as the world seemed to tilt beneath me.

"I thought... I thought you were dead." The words trembled from my lips, scarcely louder than a whisper. My gaze clung to hers, searching, doubting, and then surrendering to the truth etched into her face. Time had shaped her features—sharper now, weathered by wind and salt—but the soul of her, the girl I had grown up with, was unmistakable.

Five years had passed, and yet here she was, alive and laying below me. My voice softened as the weight of it all settled in my chest. "You remembered your promise?" My question was laden with something fragile. "How did you even know it was my wedding day?"

"Was that today?" Her grin was sharp, yet laced with a playfulness that tugged at buried memories. "That explains why you're wearing this god-awful dress." She released her grip on me, her hand emerging from the tangled folds of satin and lace to pluck the dagger from my grasp. Her touch was deliberate, almost gentle, as she dropped the blade aside. It clattered to the floor with a sound that seemed to echo endlessly. "Of course I remembered." Her expression softened, her eyes glinting with something achingly familiar. "I always keep my promises."

The words struck me deeply, their weight pressing against years of longing and loss. Slowly, I pulled myself off her, gathering the shroud of my wedding gown as I sat beside her. She shifted to sit with me.

"What happened, Maura? All those years ago... why..." My voice wavered, and the storm brewing in me spilled over into my words. "Five years, Maura... It's been five years. I needed you. Where were you?"

Her expression faltered, regret dimming her spark. "Clearly I'm not the first Captain Erius," she began, her voice quiet, each word carefully measured. "The name is a legend—older than you and me, older than most who sail these seas. It gets passed down, and a year ago, it passed to me. The man before me, Roberto Westbeys, came to Florwyn five years ago. They were looking for something—someone." Her voice caught, the hesitation palpable. "I wasn't taken, Ahrin. I... I stowed away."

The air fled my lungs as her words struck home. She left me. *Willingly.*

I rose to my feet, the sudden movement heavy with the anger that unfurled in my chest like a storm cloud. My gaze swept across the room, taking in the shelves brimming with journals, maps curling at the edges, crates spilling with treasure. The trappings of a pirate's life—a life at sea.

"You left me," I said, my voice barely above a breath, trembling with the rage and betrayal that coursed through me. My fingers brushed over the leather sheath of her sword where it rested on the desk. Its hilt was worn, weathered by years of use. She left me for this—for the lure of the open sea and freedom. I couldn't decide what angered me more: that she had abandoned me without a second thought, or that if our roles had been reversed, I knew I would have done the same. For five years, she had been living the dream we once shared, while I had been left behind, drowning in solitude and expectation.

"I grieved you," I said, the confession heavier than the weight of her absence.

"I know,"

"You abandoned me." The words fractured as they left me, splintered by the tears I fought to suppress.

"I know."

The bed creaked as she stood, her presence a shadow that loomed behind me. Still, I couldn't bring myself to look at her.

"If I could've come back sooner, I would have," she said, her voice quieter now, tinged with something close to pleading. "They didn't exactly welcome a stowaway. They weren't going to let me walk away alive, Ahrin. I had to fight for my place, claw my way to survival. And now, I'm here. I came back for you."

Her arms encircled me then, warm and firm, turning me gently until we faced each other. Her gaze held mine, raw and unyielding. "I'm here now," she repeated, her voice breaking on the words. "And I am very sorry."

Her apology shattered something within me, and I hated how it also began to piece me back together. But for now, I let myself stand in her arms, between the fury of the past and the fragile hope of the present, unsure if I could ever forgive her—or if I even wanted to.

Chapter Two

Three Days to Sail Free

We emerged onto the upper deck, where dawn draped the ocean in deepening hues of cobalt, the horizon set aflame with gold and amber. A breeze carried the brine-laden scent of the sea, teasing loose strands of my hair. The clothes Maura had given me—a blouse and trousers—hung loose in places, their rough fabric unfamiliar against my skin. Yet I found some comfort in the way they allowed me to move freely, unburdened by layers of tulle and lace.

"Apologies it's not silk," Maura quipped as she adjusted the cuffs of her coat. "But your dress will be waiting for you anytime you feel like suffocating in it again."

I rolled my eyes, tracing my fingers along the weathered railing before leaning into its support. The ship stretched vast before me, larger than any vessel in Zostera's fleet. Though its sails and rigging were the same as any ship meant to brave the high seas, it exuded an unpolished charm, its decks alive with purpose rather than perfection. The crew moved as though the ocean was their dance partner—fluid, instinctive. It stood in stark contrast to the rigid, drilled movements of naval men who obeyed orders without question. One sought to tame the sea; the other seemed to embrace it.

"Come," Maura called, jerking her head toward the quarterdeck. "Time to meet the crew."

I followed her up the steps, my attention quickly drawn to a familiar figure standing behind the helm. Bran.

"You've already met," Maura said, a smile tugging at her lips. "But let's make it formal. Bran, my first mate, this is Ahrin, my best friend. Ahrin, Bran."

Bran offered a lazy nod, his hands resting easily on the wheel.

"Do you often masquerade as captain?" I asked, crossing my arms over my chest.

"That," he said with a shrug, "was entirely the captain's idea."

"I needed the guards focused on him," Maura explained, leaning casually against the railing. "Everyone assumes the biggest, loudest person in the room is in charge. That allowed me to come up behind you unnoticed. Besides," she added with a faint smirk, "I don't exactly strike people as a threat."

It was her. I swallowed hard, my jaw tightening as anger began to simmer. "You held a firearm to the back of my head," I said, my voice low and trembling with suppressed fury. The memory, sharp and vivid, surged through me, and my fists curled at my sides. "What's wrong with you?"

She stepped closer, her fingers forming the shape of a pistol. I instinctively took a step back, but her hand shot out to grip my arm, anchoring me in place. Standing beside me now, she raised her hand, pressing her fingers lightly to the back of my head.

"This is what you felt," her tone even. "Perception, Ahrin. I would never truly put you in harm's way."

Our eyes locked, hers steady and unyielding. A challenge lingered in the silence between us, and though her hand dropped back to her side, the tension remained.

"All that matters," she continued, her lips curling into a humorless smile, "is that you believed it. They believed it."

"And now the entire kingdom thinks I've been taken by pirates," I shot back, frustration creeping into my voice. "You realize they'll stop at nothing to find me?"

"We're well aware," Maura said with a sigh. "Your father has already sent a fleet."

I turned away from her, gesturing toward the ship, the crew, the chaos she had brought into my life. "What's the plan here, Maura? Drag us both into exile? You should've come back as yourself, without all... this."

"And what then?" she asked, her voice rising with sharpness. "'Sorry, Father, but instead of going to Thalassia with Jasper, I've decided to take a sabbatical aboard my childhood best friend's pirate ship. Don't wait up.'" She scoffed, shaking her head. "No, Ahrin. It wouldn't have mattered if I'd been honest. They'd have dragged you back to that altar anyway."

She stepped closer, her voice softening as she looked me in the eye. "I made you a promise," she said, her words laced with quiet conviction. "And I always keep my promises."

I couldn't argue with that notion—Maura had always kept her word. It was a trait she'd inherited from her father, a man known for his unwavering honor. That unyielding sense of duty was why my father had entrusted him with a captaincy in the Navy. It was through that bond between our fathers that Maura and I had first crossed paths, though neither of us could have predicted how deeply intertwined our lives would become.

I hadn't had many friends growing up. The daughters of court ladies were often wolves in silk, eager to feign closeness either to capture my brothers' attention or to boast about their proximity to royalty. But Maura was different.

We hadn't liked each other at first. Our conversations were barbed, arguments over the logistics of ships and the placement of starboard devolving into petty competitions, each of us desperate to one-up the other. Yet, over time, those quarrels softened. Beneath the surface, we recognized how alike we were: two restless souls yearning for more than what society prescribed. A friendship rooted in fiery determination and shared dreams began to bloom.

"Captain."

The voice that broke through my thoughts was quiet, almost melodic. I turned to see a young man approaching. His features were soft, untouched by the rough winds and hardened edges that marked most of the crew. His ash-blond hair framed a face so open, it was almost disarming, and his emerald eyes carried a depth that suggested he saw more than he let on.

"Malachi," Maura greeted him warmly, resting a hand on his broad shoulder. "Perfect timing." She gestured toward me. "This is Malachi, our navigator and resident explosives enthusiast."

"Explosives?" I arched a brow, intrigued. "Are you the one responsible for the smoke that filled the great hall?"

"That would be me, yes, Your Highness," he replied with a humble dip of his head.

"They worked perfectly," Bran interjected with a laugh. "The smoke rose fast but stayed low enough for us to keep our bearings. If you could replicate that effect out in the open, it'd make dealing with sirens a hell of a lot easier."

"You've encountered sirens?" My breath hitched, my words tumbling out before I could catch myself. "I thought they were only found in the Dead Sea. Why were you there?"

The Dead Sea—a name that sent a chill through even the most seasoned sailors. Its treacherous waters were littered with jagged outcroppings, its skies prone to sudden, merciless storms. It was said the sea gods themselves guarded its secrets, sending sirens to lure any foolhardy mortals to their doom.

"There's so much ocean out there," Maura replied with a trace of amusement, "one gets curious about the places no one dares to tread."

"We didn't venture far," Malachi added. "We just wanted to see how far the edges of the Dead Sea stretched. But once the sirens noticed us, we turned back. If my smoke bombs worked better in open spaces... Well without their sight, their spell weakens."

"A siren's song pulls you toward them, tempts you to draw closer," Maura said, securing her long brown hair beneath her hat. "But it's their eyes that truly bind you. Look into them, and you're lost."

A shiver crawled up my spine, but Maura quickly waved the topic away. "Enough about monsters," she said. "Let's head below deck."

I glanced back at Malachi, offering him a polite smile. "It was a pleasure to meet you."

"And you, Your Highness," he replied, a flicker of curiosity lighting his gaze.

Following Maura below deck, I met several more members of her crew, each of them polite and surprisingly deferential. This wasn't what I'd been told to expect from pirates. My father and the Navy men spoke of them as brutes—barbarians ruled by lust and blood, their manners as rough as the seas they sailed.

But these sailors? They felt more like a family. Ordinary men, bonded by a shared purpose. They worked hard, spoke with respect, and moved with the ease of people who knew and trusted one another. In fact, I'd endured more wandering eyes and crude remarks from the castle guards back home than I had from anyone aboard this ship.

I startled, a yelp escaping my lips at the sensation of something warm brushing against my leg. Glancing down, I was met with a bundle of black and white fur, its small body winding affectionately around my ankle. The sound of a soft purr rose above the hum of conversation in the mess deck. For a moment, the men around us turned their curious gazes toward me, but they soon returned to their meals, their chatter weaving back into the rhythm of the ship.

"You have a cat on board?" I crouched, my fingers tentatively sinking into the silken fur. The creature leaned into my touch, its purr growing louder, a contented vibration beneath my hand.

"That would be Mr. Wiggles." Maura's voice carried a note of laughter, low and fond. She knelt beside me, her fingers sliding beneath the cat's chin, coaxing an even deeper purr from him. "We found him outside a tavern we docked at, rummaging through the chum buckets."

"Mr. Wiggles?" I raised a brow, my lips curving in spite of myself. "Why that name?"

"Because..." Maura's voice dipped into a playful cadence as she scratched under his chin, the cat's body swaying slightly in bliss. "He wiggles."

Her smile was a soft thing, catching the lamplight of the mess deck as she shifted to pet the cat's back. Her hand brushed against mine—just briefly—but the touch sparked something quiet and aching within me. It reminded me of the simplicity of moments like this, moments I hadn't known I missed until now. For years, my life had been a parade of expectations: discussions of duty, of Jasper, of the wedding, of everything I was meant to become.

"Maura," I murmured, pulling my hand away. "I can't stay here."

Her hand stilled against the cat's fur. "Why not?"

"I have obligations."

"You mean," she said, straightening as her voice turned sharper, more pointed, "you have a husband you're expected to live in the shadow of."

The words cut deeper than I cared to admit. They were my own words, spoken long ago when we were girls. Back then, I'd clung to the notion embedded in me that a wife's duty was to stand beside her husband, to support his triumphs, to bring him more success by being beautiful and obedient, by bearing his children. For some, that was enough—a life of quiet fulfillment. I had once convinced myself it would be enough for me, too, though it never had. Others assured me I would feel differently when I fell in love, but love had remained an elusive thing, a whisper in the distance I could never grasp.

"Stay with me," she said, her voice softening. "We could finally live the life we dreamed of, Ahrin. Together."

I shook my head, though I felt the faintest pull at her words, a ghost of a wish I had tried to bury time and time again. "It's not that simple. Not for me. You know that."

The weight of my station, the consequences of my absence—they hung over me like storm clouds. Maura had defied her father's plans for her, but I wasn't afforded that luxury. My life wasn't my own; my choices were threads woven into the fabric of my family, my kingdom and now Thalassia.

"Besides," I added, more quietly, "my dreams have changed."

Her gaze lingered on me, searching, as though she could see the truth beneath my words. Then she rose, her movements deliberate, her expression unreadable.

"Give me three days," she said. "Three days to remind you of what you used to want, what we used to dream of."

"Three days," I echoed, the words tentative on my tongue. "Fine. I'll give you that. But you have to promise me, Maura—if I still choose to return to Zostera after those three days, you'll take me back. Swear it."

Her voice dropped to a whisper, the sound barely reaching me over the creak of the ship. "I promise."

Chapter Three

The Heave and the Ho

"Where are we?" I asked, raising my hand to shield my eyes as the island came into view, its silhouette growing larger against the shimmer of the open sea. The sunlight turned the waves into golden threads, their soft whispers lapping at the hull as we drew nearer.

"Piscia Isle," Malachi said, his tone casual as he strode past with a crate balanced effortlessly in his grip. "It's well beyond Zostera's jurisdiction, and even if it wasn't, the lord here doesn't care for King Caldwell's decrees. Makes it an ideal place to lose a naval pursuit."

"A safe haven for us," Maura added, her voice laced with a quiet confidence as she joined us at the railing. "And a perfect chance to show you what life at sea can offer—the places, the people. The freedom."

I didn't miss the subtle lure in her words, the gentle invitation to step further into her world. Yet even as I tried to remind myself of my obligations, excitement stirred in my chest. I had never left Zostera. My life had been hemmed in by its borders, its ports a promise never fulfilled. My brothers had tasted freedom, each in their own way: Tae following my father into the navy, and Ryung forging his path in the military. But for me, the world remained distant, a story told by others.

As we docked, the crew moved with the rhythm of familiarity, their work seamless as they settled the ship into its brief reprieve. I followed Maura and the others down the gangplank, the wood creaking softly beneath our steps.

There were no grand markets or bustling squares here, only modest stalls and makeshift shops run by those who had chosen this place as their home. The dirt roads did not merely carve paths through the land—they coexisted with it, worn smooth by time and reverence. Piscia Isle seemed to exist in a liminal state, neither thriving nor fading, a resting ground for sailors who sought refuge between journeys. Quiet, humble and enduring.

"Wait until nightfall," Maura said, her gaze sweeping the docks as she adjusted her hat. The sun caught the brown strands of her hair as she gathered them deftly into her hand, tucking them beneath the brim. "That's when the island comes alive. The liquor flows, the music rises, and men spend their coin for a fleeting taste of joy."

It was then I noticed it—a mark at the base of her neck, just visible in the sunlight. The tattoo, inked in bold lines, matched the one Bran and the others bore. The mark of Erius.

Maura caught me staring, her hand brushing over the ink as though it were a reflex. "This," she said, her tone light yet deliberate, "earns us respect among the folk outside the continent. I make sure to display it. It tells them who we are and where we belong." She let her fingers drop, her attention shifting briefly to my hair, which hung loose around my shoulders. "I also like having my hair up because it's practical too. Long hair and beards are easy targets when things turn... less than civil."

Her hand reached out, her fingers weaving gently through a strand of my dark locks. "I know you hate tying it back, but we'll find something to keep it out of your eyes. Just in case."

She turned then, her voice carrying a note of command as she spoke to Bran. "Make sure all is settled with Lord Dedric. I'll show Ahrin around. Meet us at the Fin and Flagon when you're done."

With a nod, Bran and the others veered away, leaving Maura and me to navigate the winding docks.

"What did you mean by 'settled'?" I asked as curiosity tugged at me. "I thought you said your name was respected here."

"It is," she replied, her tone calm, almost amused. "But respect, once earned, must be maintained. We trade for them—goods they can't grow or make themselves. The island's livelihood doesn't run on sailors' coin alone."

"Isn't that the navy's duty?" I pressed. "To handle trade between the continent and the Perpelagust Isles?"

"For a price," she said with a dry chuckle. "And most naval guards treat these people like vermin, seeing them as less for living outside the crown's reach. Besides," she added, her gaze shifting toward the island's modest bustle, "gold isn't the only currency here. And the crown despises what it cannot control."

Her words brought to mind the palace councils I'd overheard, their voices sharp with disdain for barter systems and islands like this. To them, anything that disrupted the flow of coin was a threat to the kingdom's evolving economy. Yet there was something old and honest about trade in its simplest form, something that tugged at my understanding of right and wrong.

"I suppose it is the way of things here," I said softly

Maura glanced at me, her smile faint but knowing. "You'll see soon enough, Ahrin. Sometimes the world outside the crown is more balanced than you think."

"Ooh, this way." Maura's hand slipped into mine, warm and firm, tugging me along at a pace that matched the lightness in her step. A playful smile curved her lips, her excitement infectious.

"I know it's nothing like the grand shops of Zostera," she said, her voice tinged with affection, "but every time I've come here, I thought of you."

She led me down a narrow stretch of the docks to a humble shop nestled between weathered warehouses and fishing stalls. The sign above the wide, open doors read Seafarer's Stitch, the letters carved into wood worn smooth by the salt-laden air. A sea breeze wove through the entryway, carrying the faint scent of salt and the tang of freshly hewn timber.

Inside, the shop was a quiet haven of warmth and craft. Bolts of fabric in earthy tones and jewel hues were draped over wooden racks, their edges fraying artfully. Dresses and bodices hung along the walls, their designs understated but meticulous. Each piece seemed a labor of love, the stitching precise, the fabrics chosen not for opulence but for the way they spoke to the wearer.

My fingers trailed over a bodice of soft green linen, the texture cool against my skin. "These are beautiful," I murmured, not out of politeness but with genuine awe. The dresses were simple, their charm in the elegance of their cut and the care given to every detail. They were nothing like the layered, gem-encrusted gowns of court, yet they struck a chord in me that those grand creations never had.

I found myself drawn to a dress of deep indigo, its bodice as black as a midnight sea. The stitching along the seams was so fine it seemed woven from moonlight.

"I knew you'd find something here." Maura's voice was soft, her smile a quiet triumph as her fingers brushed the fabric beside mine. "Lina does exceptional work."

"Lina?" I asked, glancing up.

"That would be me," a voice chimed, lilting and smooth. A woman approached, about our age, her beauty understated and her gown as finely crafted as those on display. Her accent was one I couldn't place, but it lent an exotic quality to her presence, adding to the quiet allure she exuded.

"These pieces are exquisite," I said, meaning every word. "Do you have any idea how much you could make if you brought these to the continent?"

"Mm, but then I'd have to charge far more gold," Lina said softly, her fingers deftly adjusting the hem of a nearby dress. "The resources to craft these would cost a fortune on the continent."

"And we couldn't have that," Maura chimed, her tone light with playful warmth. "Where else would the women of the Perpelagust Sea find gowns as fine as yours?"

"True," Lina replied with a sly smile, her gaze flicking to Maura. "Besides, I'm fairly certain you're not welcome on the continent. And I'd miss you terribly if I left."

Maura laughed, a low and genuine sound that softened the air between them.

I turned back to the dress in my hands, my fingers brushing the fabric almost reverently. "I'd like to purchase this," I said, only to remember, with a flush of embarrassment, that I had no coin. My hands fell to my trousers as I sighed softly. "But I—"

"I've got it," Maura interrupted, her voice firm. "And anything else you'd like for your time with me." She looked to

Lina. "Would you fit her in this one? And gather a few others in similar styles for us to pick up tomorrow?"

"Right away, Captain." Lina's voice softened into something akin to a purr as she took the dress from my hands and led me to a private corner of the shop.

Her movements were fluid, practiced, as she took my measurements and adjusted the gown to fit me. I watched her work in the mirror, marveling at her quiet efficiency and the subtle artistry of her hands.

"I'll tailor the other dresses to this size," Lina said, stepping back to inspect her work. She moved to a rack of ribbons, pulling one free with practiced ease. "Maura mentioned you prefer your hair loose, but she thought you might need something to keep it from your face. Let's see."

She gathered the sides of my hair, weaving them back with the ribbon until the style was both practical and elegant.

"Maura," she called, and within moments, Maura appeared, slipping through the curtain with a soft rustle.

Her gaze softened as she took me in, her eyes lingering as though memorizing every detail. "This suits you," she murmured, stepping closer to adjust a strand of hair, letting it fall to frame my face. "There. Now it's *you*."

For a moment, her eyes locked with mine, and I felt the weight of her attention settle on me, intimate and unguarded. It was only then that I noticed the faint scar on her face—one tracing over the bridge of her nose. Time and care had softened it, but it remained.

Breaking the moment, I smoothed my hands along the bodice and down the skirt, letting the soft fabric ground me. "Thank you," I said, glancing at Lina. "You truly should consider opening a shop in Zostera. It's a shame more people don't see your work."

Lina smiled, a faint blush rising to her cheeks. "Perhaps one day," she said, her voice as gentle as the sea breeze outside.

Maura was right—the island truly came alive as night fell. Piscia Isle shed its quiet, rustic demeanor, transforming into something almost magical under the embrace of twilight. The sea, now a vast sheet of molten silver, mirrored the first stars that scattered across the heavens. The setting sun bled into the horizon, its last rays gilding the island's sands and the lanterns that flickered to life along the docks. The air grew cooler, carrying the salt of the sea and the faint, bittersweet tang of ale from the tavern up ahead.

The Fin and Flagon loomed larger than any other structure I'd seen here, its weathered facade exuding a strange sort of grandeur amid the modest surroundings. Warm light spilled through its wide windows, accompanied by a medley of laughter, raucous conversation, and the faint strum of a lute.

The sound grew louder as we approached, weaving itself into the very pulse of the island.

"This is their crown jewel," Maura explained, pushing open the door. "Most of the island's coin comes from this place—booze downstairs, gambling upstairs. Not a bad setup if you don't mind parting with your gold."

As we stepped inside, I felt the weight of countless eyes on us. Conversations dipped, and I caught more than a few assessing glances thrown my way. Though I stood tall, I couldn't shake the feeling of being hopelessly out of place in their world, like a fine porcelain vase set down in a room of rough, sea-worn treasures.

The tavern was alive with energy—a chaotic swirl of sound and movement. The tables were crowded with sailors and merchants, their faces flushed from drink, their voices rising in lively debate or bawdy songs. Walking the wooden floors, the serving wenches with their ample curves accentuated and voices honeyed, revealed just enough skin to coax the drunken into parting with their coin. Smoke from a nearby pipe curled through the air, mingling with the scent of spiced rum and roasted meat. Lanterns hung from wooden beams, casting flickering shadows that danced across walls adorned with faded nautical maps and weathered trinkets from far-off shores.

"Captain! Ahrin! Over here!" Bran's voice called from the corner.

The crew had claimed several tables near the back, a loud, boisterous gathering that seemed impervious to the chaos around them. I followed Maura's lead, sliding onto a bench beside Bran as a tankard of ale was set before me. I turned to see Malachi standing there, his dark eyes glinting with a quiet greeting.

"Thank you," I murmured, offering him a small smile.

He hesitated, as though weighing something unsaid, before his voice came soft and sincere. "You look beautiful, Your Highness."

A warmth bloomed in my cheeks, catching me off guard, and I shifted to make room for him beside me. As he sat, the low hum of the crew's laughter and stories enveloped us, and I found myself drawn into their camaraderie. They spoke of storms survived, treasures won and lost, and the strange, distant lands they'd glimpsed on the horizon.

The ale was far from the fine vintages I was used to—it was bitter and rough, leaving an almost metallic taste on my tongue. Yet with each sip, the sharpness softened, becoming something oddly comforting, something that belonged in this world of theirs.

Their closeness was palpable, woven into every teasing remark, every knowing glance shared across the table. They were more than a crew—they were a family. It stirred something raw and unfamiliar within me, a pang of longing for a bond I had never known.

"Are you all right?" Maura leaned in to whisper, her voice cutting through the haze of my thoughts.

"Yes," I replied quickly, though my voice wavered. "I think I just want another drink, if that's all right."

Maura arched a brow but nodded, a hint of a smile playing on her lips. "Careful now. I don't imagine you've had much experience with alcohol." She turned to the barkeep with a wave. "Another round over here!"

The crew cheered in unison, raising their tankards in anticipation.

"Believe it or not," Maura began, her voice light with mischief, "The princess had a rebellious streak in her youth. She used to sneak into Zostera's naval base to steal their maps."

I laughed softly, shaking my head at the memory. "I always returned them—after making copies, of course."

"You made copies?" Malachi leaned closer, his interest piqued. "You have a knack for cartography, then?"

"I... I suppose," I stammered, caught off guard by the intensity of his gaze. "Maps fascinate me. They show you things."

"That they do," he said, his tone thoughtful as he smiled gently.

"I mean, they're more than just ink on parchment; they're stories of the world, waiting to be read."

"That is true. I too like that about them." Malachi said. "What medium do you prefer for your work? I always found vellum the finest, though regular parchment will do in a pinch."

"Vellum too," I said, a touch too eagerly. "Nothing compares to the smoothness of calfskin for detailed work."

"Calfskin?" He chuckled, his expression warm. "An odd way to phrase it, but I suppose you're right."

"Ahrin," Maura interrupted with a playful grin, "let me show you how to properly order a drink at a tavern. We'll be back."

I followed her reluctantly, casting a glance over my shoulder at Malachi. His eyes lingered on me for a moment longer before he turned back to the others, his smile still soft on his lips.

"What are you doing?" Maura spoke hushly, pulling me into the shadow of a doorway. Her sharp, knowing eyes studied me, her amusement barely concealed.

"I don't know," I whispered, my voice cracking under the weight of my nerves. "I've never talked to a boy before—besides Jasper, I mean."

Her laugh was soft. "First of all, Malachi isn't a boy. He's a man." She smirked, leaning in conspiratorially. "And secondly, you need to remember who you are, Ahrin. You're a princess—hot, untouchable, and far too good to be nervous over some pirate. Look at him."

She tilted her head toward the corner, where Malachi sat. I dared to peek around the edge, my breath catching as I watched him. He fiddled with the collar of his shirt, tugging at the fabric as though it suddenly felt too tight, his other hand raking through his unruly hair in quick, nervous strokes.

"See?" Maura whispered, her voice brimming with satisfaction. "Look how nervous you've made him—just the thought of you has him in knots."

I blinked, torn between disbelief and a strange sort of thrill. Malachi did look unsettled, almost shy in a way that mirrored my own awkwardness. But if he was nervous, I was a hurricane—a storm of doubt and clumsiness. I felt utterly foolish, out of my depth in every possible way, while Maura radiated a calm, effortless confidence that only magnified my inadequacy. She seemed to move through the world with a grace I could only dream of possessing.

She caught me staring at her, and her brows knit together. "What?"

"Nothing," I said quickly, though the words tumbled out unconvincingly. I dropped my gaze, heat blooming in my cheeks. "I just... I wish I were more like you. More experienced."

"You really like him, don't you?"

"Yes." The word slipped from my lips like the faintest breeze, weightless yet laden with the unspoken. It wasn't a simple admission. It wasn't simple at all. I barely knew Malachi—his voice, his laugh, the curve of his lips when he smiled. But what little I did know tugged at something deep within me, something that had been dormant and waiting.

He embodied a dream I hadn't realized I'd nurtured in the quiet corners of my heart. A man who didn't just exist beside me but shared in my passions, who could explore the vast seas of thought and ambition as eagerly as the maps he sketched. I wanted to learn him like I would a coastline—every curve, every hidden inlet, every treacherous reef that marked his soul.

But even as the thought warmed me, I sighed, the weight of doubt anchoring my hope. "I can't even manage a proper conversation with him. I stumble over my words, and that's just talking. I can't imagine..." My voice faltered, and my gaze drifted toward him once more.

"He's..." I hesitated, a blush creeping to my cheeks. "He's cute. His lips look... soft."

Her lips curved into a sly smile, a memory sparking in her eyes. "Do you remember when we practiced kissing on our hands? And then you suggested we kiss each other, just so you could make sure you weren't terrible for Jasper?"

The memory hit me like a gust of warm wind, and my face flushed deeper. "Y-Yes," I stuttered, suddenly wishing the ground beneath us would open and swallow me whole.

Maura leaned in closer, her voice dropping to a low, soothing murmur. "Remember this, Ahrin: it's all about leaning in." She lifted a finger, gently tilting my chin upward, her gaze steady and intent. My breath caught as her eyes flickered down to my lips, the space between us so slight it felt like her words were brushing against me.

"Lean," she instructed, her voice calm and measured, a counterpoint to the chaos thundering in my chest. "Press your lips—lightly, just enough—and then pull back. Slow. Let it linger."

She demonstrated the motion as she spoke, the curve of her lips barely brushing mine, ghosting over them in a whisper of air. My heart tripped over itself, her breath warm and fleeting, and I felt more unsteady than ever.

"And then," she said softly, her finger retreating from my chin as her eyes locked with mine, "you just let your body do the rest. No words needed."

The space between us filled with silence, heavy and charged. I swallowed hard, trying to compose myself as she casually lifted her tankard to her lips, her nonchalance only making the moment cling tighter to my skin.

"Let my body do the rest," I repeated, the words barely audible as I worked to steady my trembling hands.

She smiled, her confidence a beacon I wished I could reach. "You've got this." Her hand nudged me forward, a gentle push that felt like a command.

I took a deep breath and stepped toward Malachi, her words still hanging in the air, her presence still haunting my lips.

"Where's the Captain?" Malachi asked, his curiosity softening the edges of his deep voice. He glanced around, his gaze settling on me as I took my seat beside him. Most of the crew had dispersed, some returning to the bar, others vanishing upstairs to try their luck at cards or dice.

"She said she needed to speak with Bran about something. I... forgot what exactly," I replied, the words coming out a little too quick, too airy. My fingers fidgeted with the edge of my tankard. "So, it's just us, then," I added with a smile I hoped didn't betray the storm of nerves battering against my composure.

The silence that followed was a heavy thing, stretching between us like the endless expanse of the sea. My thoughts raced, every second making the air feel thicker, harder to breathe. *Now or never, Ahrin,* I told myself.

I leaned forward before doubt could anchor me, my palm trembling as it came to rest against the warmth of his cheek. Closing my eyes, I pressed my lips to his, the motion tentative and unpracticed. He stilled beneath my touch, and for a fleeting moment, panic seized me. Had I rushed things?

But then, his hand rose to mirror mine, his palm cradling the curve of my face as he closed the distance once more. His lips moved against mine, firmer now, guiding me with an ease that made me dizzy.

Just as Maura had said, I let my body take the reins, surrendering to instinct as I pressed closer. My head tilted slightly, the kiss deepening as the faintest brush of his tongue sent a shiver down my spine.

What would Maura do?

The thought flared unbidden, unrelenting. I parted my lips further, meeting his tentative touch with my own, our tongues moving in a rhythm I hoped was right. A silent, desperate question echoed through me: *Is this how she would do it? Is this how she would like it?*

And then, suddenly, Malachi pulled back, his hand falling away as his brows furrowed. His expression held confusion, maybe even a touch of hurt. "Maura?" he asked, his voice quiet but pointed.

"What?" The word left me in a breathless rush, though the heat rising to my face was impossible to ignore.

"You said Maura."

"No, I didn't." The denial tumbled out too quickly, too sharp, but the widening of his eyes told me I'd been caught. Had

I really said her name? My mind scrambled, replaying every second, and yet the truth eluded me.

"You did," he said, his tone edged with disbelief. He shifted away, creating a gap between us that felt wider than the ocean itself, his thigh no longer brushing mine. Reaching for his tankard, he took a long, deliberate sip, leaving the silence between us colder than it had been before.

A wave of nausea swept over me, rising swiftly from the pit of my stomach and curling into my throat. My head spun, the room tilting as shame twisted its claws deep into my chest.

"Are you okay?" he asked, his voice distant, like it was coming from the other side of a storm. "You don't look so well."

"I—I just need some air," I managed, stumbling to my feet and nearly knocking over a chair in my haste.

The moment I stepped outside, the crisp night air struck me like a slap. It did little to calm the roiling in my stomach. Gripping the wooden railing of the balcony, I leaned over just as the sickness surged, emptying the contents of my stomach onto the sands below.

My hair was pulled back gently, a hand smoothing down my back in soothing circles. Her touch was familiar, grounding. "Well," Maura said, her voice low and tinged with playful amusement, "at least you didn't puke in his mouth. That would have been a far worse story for the crew to tell."

I let out a weak, miserable groan, my body trembling from the exertion.

"This is enough rebelling for you tonight, princess," she continued, her tone softening, though the teasing edge remained. "Come on. Let me walk you back to the ship."

Chapter Four

Calm Before the Storm

Maura's hands glided up my thighs, her touch slow and deliberate, lifting the hem of my dress with unspoken intent. Her fingers lingered at my waist, pulling me gently onto her lap. One hand claimed the curve of my backside while the other wove into my hair, her grip firm yet tender as she guided my lips to hers. Her mouth was soft, warm, and intoxicatingly sure.

My own hands wandered, tentative at first, then bolder, trailing up her body until one cupped the swell of her breast. Her breath hitched against my lips, and my heart thundered in response. Our tongues met, a tantalizing dance that left me breathless. A heat bloomed between my thighs, sharp and undeniable, as her lips drifted to the hollow of my neck, planting kisses that sent shivers racing down my spine.

She murmured something against my skin, her voice low and teasing, the words lost to me.

"Hmm?" I managed, barely coherent.

She pulled back just enough for our eyes to meet, her expression one of mischievous delight. Then, absurdly, she meowed.

She meowed?

The sound reverberated in my mind, twisting the dream as reality came crashing in. I jolted awake to a very different warmth—one that pressed insistently against my chest, accompanied by a wave of queasiness that wiped the remnants of sleep from my mind.

Peeling my eyes open, I found a black-and-white fluffball sprawled atop me, its tiny weight a surprising anchor. Mr. Wiggles.

It was just a dream.

His soft purring rumbled through my chest like a distant storm, and I couldn't help but reach out to stroke his fur. He leaned into the touch, utterly content, as though my chest was his rightful throne.

The nausea surged suddenly, sharp and unyielding. Gently but hastily, I lifted Mr. Wiggles and deposited him onto the bed beside me. Then I bolted upright, the unsettling churn in my stomach demanding my full attention as I braced myself against the consequences of last night.

"There's a bucket at your feet—please don't—" Maura's voice broke off, eclipsed by the sharp sound of retching as I lurched forward and heaved into the bucket. The acid burn of bile clawed up my throat, each convulsion echoing with a dull throb in my head. My body trembled under the onslaught, fragile and humiliated.

"Why..." I croaked, sinking to the floor with the bucket clutched against me like a shield. "Why do people drink if it leads to this?" My voice faltered as I pressed my back against the wooden wall, gaze flicking upward to meet Maura's.

She was perched on the edge of the bed, the soft morning light framing her like an artist's dream. Mr. Wiggles rested contentedly in her lap, purring as her fingers combed through his fur. She looked unbothered, radiant even, her unruly curls cascading in a wild halo. The warm honey of her skin glowed as if untouched by the revelry of the night before.

And there I sat, a wretched heap on the floor, utterly dwarfed by her poise. "Why do you look so well? Did you not drink?" I mumbled, my voice hoarse.

"I did. We all did," she replied, her lips curling into a teasing smile. "The difference is, we're accustomed to it. You, on the other hand—when was the last time you touched a drop of spirits?"

"When we snuck into the cellar after curfew that one night."

"That was six years ago, Ahrin," she said with a playful sigh, shaking her head as though she pitied my naivety.

My mother's laws of decorum had stripped me of indulgence, spirits among them. Purity, she called it—a virtue to be upheld for the sake of appearances. But I had always wondered what magic lived in the tempting liquid, what secrets it held that made it a companion to both celebration and sorrow. Even now, hunched over and broken by its aftermath, I couldn't understand why anyone willingly subjected themselves to this torment.

"Though I jest, we've all been where you are," Maura said, slipping from the bed. Her bare feet whispered against the floorboards, and for the first time, I noticed her attire—or lack of it. She wore only a loose white blouse that hung to mid-thigh, the fabric catching the light and clinging to the curves of her body. She crossed the room to the desk, pulling open a drawer and retrieving a small bottle.

Returning to me, she held it out—a glass vial filled with a pale amber liquid that swirled languidly as she tipped it side to side. "It's a tonic for hangovers," she explained, her voice tinged with the faintest note of nostalgia. "My dearest companion back when I first discovered ale."

I eyed the bottle with suspicion, its contents thick and unappealing. "It looks disgusting."

"It's willow bark, nettle, and honey," she said softly, her gaze steady on mine. "Trust me."

Her voice was a balm, but it was her presence that unraveled me. My eyes betrayed me, wandering down the line of her throat to the low neckline of her blouse. The curve of her breast drew my attention, and in an instant, the dream returned unbidden. Heat surged through me, pooling low and across my cheeks.

I scrambled to compose myself. "T-Thank you," I stammered, snatching the bottle from her hand and popping the cork. The bittersweet liquid slid down my throat, but I barely tasted it. My desperation for distraction was all-consuming.

Thankfully, she turned and returned to the bed, settling back on the edge with effortless grace. Wiggles curled against her thigh, purring his approval. I focused on the dull burn of the tonic, praying it would steady me—praying it would quiet the storm raging beneath my skin.

"Thank you again," I said, breathless, as we trudged up the steep hillside. My chest rose and fell like the tide, each inhalation a struggle against the relentless incline. "For the tonic. It truly was a lifesaver."

Without it, I doubted I'd have managed even to rise from bed, let alone embark on this climb. My legs protested every step, and though I silently cursed my decision to follow Maura's lead, I was grateful for her insistence on practical footwear. Yet, I had drawn the line at trousers. Even now, struggling up this relentless trail, I refused to part with the flowing grace of one of Lina's dresses. Trousers may have offered freedom, but they never felt like me. Even during riding lessons, I had chosen sidesaddle over confinement. At least the dress offered some semblance of elegance, even as I felt like I was dying.

"We're almost there," Maura said, her tone maddeningly unaffected, as if the climb had barely quickened her breath. Her ease, her effortless strength, annoyed me more than it should have.

"How—" I swallowed hard, catching my breath. "How are you not winded?"

She only grinned and turned to face me. "Can you hear it yet?" I stopped, letting my racing heart quiet just enough to focus on the world around me. And then I heard it—a distant, melodic roar. It cut through the rustling leaves and my labored breathing.

The waterfall.

"We'll unpack a little ways from it," Maura said, shifting the satchel on her shoulder as she scanned the path ahead. "But I promise, you'll still have the perfect view."

As we climbed higher, the sound grew louder, a symphony of rushing water and the faint cries of tropical birds. When the falls came into view, I stopped in my tracks, the air caught in my lungs. Cascading water poured over jagged cliffs, shimmering in the sunlight like liquid glass. Mist rose in a delicate veil, catching rainbows in its folds. All around, the landscape was lush with life—vibrant flowers in impossible shades of red and gold bloomed against the emerald expanse of ferns and vines. From this height, I could see the village below as it was reduced to a patchwork of quiet civilization.

"Beautiful" felt like a woeful understatement. This was magical.

We reached a clearing near the falls, where Maura set down her satchel and spread a linen blanket over the soft ground. She moved with ease, her motions unhurried but purposeful.

"I haven't done this in ages," she said, her voice carrying a casual warmth as she began unpacking the satchel. A loaf of sweetened bread, a small wedge of cheese, a flask of something undoubtedly stronger than water—all set neatly upon the blanket. "My crew's never one for stopping to admire the view. They'd rather dive straight into the water."

I laughed softly, settling onto the blanket beside her. "We could enjoy the scenery and dive in," I offered. "Though that might require a change of clothes, which I doubt either of us thought to bring."

"We could just leave our clothes here," she suggested, her voice light with mischief.

I froze, feeling a warmth creep up my face. "Someone could come looking for us," I said quickly, my voice betraying more nerves than I intended.

"It's just an option," she replied with a soft chuckle, her gaze sparkling as she leaned back on her palms, entirely at ease. "But, for the record, I don't think anyone would come looking for us."

Her words lingered in the air, teasing me as much as the warmth of the sun and the hypnotic rush of water. I looked away, feigning interest in the falls, but my heart beat faster than ever. *Had she always been like this?* Her gestures, bold and unyielding, walked the precarious line between jest and vulgarity—like a sailor's, roughened by years away from courtly constraints. Perhaps she had always been this way, and it was I who had forgotten. Or perhaps it was the distance, the years that had carved an unfamiliar edge into her, that made her words stir something in me now—something I didn't know how to name.

I wasn't used to it anymore. *Yes, that had to be it.* I shifted where I sat, crossing my legs and smoothing the folds of my dress over my knees, a futile attempt to distract myself.

"We used to find spots like this to read together," Maura murmured. "I don't do much of that anymore. Reading." She reached into her satchel and withdrew a book. The cover was exquisite—a hand-painted illustration of a pale hand clutching the stem of a rose, the thorns curling like talons, while another hand gripped the wrist as though to restrain it. She extended it toward me with an almost careless grace. "I thought you might like this," she said. "Just in case you still read."

I took it gingerly, running my fingers over the textured cover. The title, *Roses de Passion*, was inscribed in curling gold script.

"It's one of those romantic stories," she added, leaning back on her hands. "The shopkeeper said they're all the rage among the nobles right now. Full of passion and intrigue."

I nodded, though words failed me for a moment. I had found myself drawn to such books in recent years—tales of daring men and devoted love, of grand gestures and whispered promises. The kind of love that would sweep me away from Zostera's unyielding shores.

"Will you read it to me?" Maura's voice softened as she slipped off her tricorn hat, letting her dark curls spill over her shoulders in a cascade of untamed beauty. She reached for her flintlock, setting it on the blanket between us like a casual afterthought. "I've missed your voice, and I've five years to make up for."

I arched a brow at her. "Make me make up for your choice to stay away?" My words were light, but bitterness laced the edges of my tone.

"You know it's more complicated than that," she sighed.

"Is it?"

Without warning, Maura leaned forward and shifted until her head was cradled in my lap, her hazel eyes gazing up at me with a softness that felt disarming. "Please, Ahrin." Her voice dipped into sweetness, the kind that made it impossible to refuse her.

I huffed, though my resolve was already crumbling. "I was going to do it anyway. No need for the dramatics."

Her smile was faint but triumphant as I opened the book, the pages faintly perfumed with ink and parchment. Yet, as I began to read, my focus wavered. Her gaze stayed fixed on me, languid and amused, while her hand drifted lazily to the hem of my dress, her fingers brushing the fabric.

My voice faltered when I reached the first explicit passage, the words slipping over my tongue like molten lead. A vivid scene of whispered confessions and stolen touches unfolded before us, and I couldn't help but fumble, heat prickling my cheeks.

"I can't," I stammered. "It's one thing to read this alone, but to read it aloud..." My voice trailed off under the weight of her knowing smile.

Maura's fingers grazed mine as she took the book from my hands, closing it with a finality that left my heart thudding. "Perhaps you should read more of these in your spare time," she teased, the corner of her mouth quirking up. "Might help you find some confidence—with Jasper, or maybe Malachi."

I groaned inwardly at the mention of Malachi. That ship had well and truly sailed without me, and Jasper? Jasper was more likely to converse with a book than with me. Perhaps passion might grow over years of marriage, but the stories whispered by older women at court suggested otherwise.

I stood abruptly, eager to change the subject. "Let's see the waterfall up close, shall we?"

My steps didn't get far before Maura's hand clasped my wrist, her touch firm enough to halt me mid-step.

"Wait," she said, her voice low enough to be lost beneath the roar of the falls.

I followed her gaze, but she wasn't looking at me. Her eyes were fixed on something in the distance, her expression sharp, her entire demeanor shifting in an instant. My breath stilled as a new tension settled between us, heavy and foreboding.

"I suppose there's no point in hiding now that you've spotted us," a gruff voice called from the shadows, its timbre deep and roughened by years at sea. A man stepped out from the dense brush, the sunlight catching on the polished barrel of the flintlock he held steady in our direction. His appearance was as rugged as his voice: wild black hair matted beneath a faded tricorne, his beard thick and streaked with gray. A jagged scar curved over his cheekbone, and clothes that spoke of long days aboard a ship and even longer nights of plunder.

Maura shifted subtly, her eyes flicking toward the firearm resting on the blanket a few paces away. The tension in her shoulders, though slight, betrayed her calculation.

"Uh-uh," came another voice from behind, sharp and sardonic. I froze as something cold and unyielding pressed into the small of my back—a blade, or perhaps the muzzle of a hand cannon. The man behind me chuckled, low and taunting, his breath hot against my ear. "I wouldn't try anything if you don't want the princess hurt."

"Maura," I breathed, my voice trembling as I dared to glance over my shoulder. The man holding me was lean but sinewy, his face weathered and creased by the sun. His nose had been broken once, perhaps twice, and his lips twisted into a smirk that revealed a gold tooth. The stink of stale rum clung to him like a second skin.

"Hey now," Maura said, her tone as cool as the sea breeze that swept through the clearing. She raised her hands slowly, deliberately, though her hazel eyes glittered with defiance. "Are you not aware of whose island you've docked on? Lord Dedric has declared this a sanctuary zone. No fighting, no bloodshed. His word is law here."

"We're aware," the first man growled, his pistol unwavering. "But we've special orders from Prince Windham of Thalassia."

At the mention of my betrothed, my stomach turned. Prince Jasper Windham must have granted these men a letter of marque, elevating them from common pirates to privateers in service of the crown.

Maura's lips curled into a wry smile, her hands still raised in mock surrender. "From pirate to privateer. My, how the mighty have fallen. Raiding merchant ships not paying what they used to, I take it?"

Her words struck like a blade, and I felt the man behind me stiffen. The leader's scarred face darkened, his grip on the flintlock tightening. Yet Maura stood unshaken, her confidence an unspoken challenge, daring them to make the first move.

Despite the hammering of my heart and the icy tremor of fear in my veins, I knew they would not harm me. At least, not outright. My value was tied to my survival. If they failed to deliver me alive, their reward would vanish. And yet... men like this were adept at weaving lies, at crafting tales of tragedy where princesses perished at the hands of villains, not their own.

"You can't be the captain," the privateer captain sneered, his gaze flicking to Maura's hat discarded on the ground, its embroidered crest of command glinting in the light. "You're just a wench playing dress-up. Where's the real captain? The one whose cock you bounce on?"

Maura's jaw tightened, but she did not flinch. Instead, her lips curved into a smile so sharp it could cut. "Even if that were true," she said, her voice smooth as silk yet laced with venom, "I much prefer women."

"Ahrin, duck!" she yelled as her hand shot to the inside of her jacket. In a single, fluid motion, she brandished a dagger.

I dropped instinctively, curling into myself, my arms shielding my head. A gurgling sound followed, wet and sickening, and when I dared to look up, I saw the man behind me clutching at his throat, Maura's blade buried deep. Blood spilled through his fingers, staining the ground as he crumpled.

The victory was short-lived. With a roar, the other lunged at Maura, tackling her to the ground. The force sent them rolling, his heavier frame pinning her beneath him. His pistol pressed against her cheek, the metal digging into her skin.

Without thinking—without knowing if it was bravery or folly driving me—I scrambled for Maura's firearm. The weight of it in my hands was unfamiliar and daunting, but I gripped it tightly, both hands trembling as I aimed at the man.

"I will shoot you," I said, my voice shaking but resolute, though my fingers quivered against the trigger.

He glanced at me, his expression a mix of amusement and scorn. "You? A little princess playing with a gun? Drop it. You'd sooner shoot yourself than hit me." His free hand wrapped around Maura's throat, squeezing, and I saw her face strain, her lips parting as she gasped for air.

The world narrowed to a single point: him, Maura, and the flintlock in my hands. The pounding of my heart was a drumbeat in my ears. I pulled the trigger.

The explosion was deafening, the recoil jarring. The bullet whizzed past his head, missing him by inches, and struck a tree behind him.

He laughed, a deep, mocking chuckle that rumbled from his chest. "Can't even aim straight," he said, shaking his head as though I were nothing more than a child fumbling with a toy.

"That," I said, forcing steel into my voice, "was a warning shot." I straightened my posture, channeling every ounce of confidence I'd ever seen in Maura. "I wouldn't want your filthy blood on my captain." The truth—that I'd aimed for his head and missed—remained locked in my chest.

He raised his hands slowly, a smirk still curling his lips. Beneath him, Maura gasped as he loosened his grip on her throat. "Alright, alright," he drawled. "How about we settle this at sea?"

He rose to his feet, stepping back from Maura with infuriating ease, as though we were part of some game he enjoyed far too much.

Maura coughed, drawing in ragged breaths, her eyes darting toward me with something that might have been gratitude—or pride. I couldn't tell, not in that moment. All I knew was that the gun still felt heavy in my trembling hands, and the threat was far from over.

Chapter Five

All Hands on Deck and Below

"Hoist the sails!" Maura's voice sliced through the brisk salt air, sharp and commanding. Her coat flared as she spun toward the mast, her movements precise and sure as though the ship itself bent to her will.

"You heard the Captain!" Bran bellowed, his voice carrying like rolling thunder. "Ready the lines, set to sail!"

Malachi fell into step beside her, his brow furrowed. "Do we know who they were?"

Maura didn't look at him, her focus sharp. "No chance to check for identifying marks," she replied, her voice taut. "They don't seem familiar, but the sea has many faces."

"And so we run?" I asked, breathless, struggling to match her relentless pace as the crew scattered to their posts.

Her head snapped toward me, a faint grin tugging at the corner of her lips, though her gaze was steely. "No," she said, her tone quiet, lethal. "They want a sea skirmish? Then we'll give them one."

The sanctuary of Piscia Isle shrank in the distance as the ship surged forward. The rhythmic snap of the sails filled the air, and the sea opened its vast arms before us, endless and unknowable. Behind us, the enemy ship loomed.

"They're holding distance," Malachi observed, his hand tightening around the hilt of his blade.

"Testing us," Maura murmured. Her eyes remained on the horizon. "They'll come. Wait for it."

As if summoned by her words, the pursuing ship drew closer, its blackened hull menacing against the relentless waves. A shout rang out from their deck, faint but clear, and ropes were loosed. Figures swung across the divide like specters in the mist.

Thuds reverberated through the deck as boots hit the planks, followed by the hiss of steel unsheathing.

"Boarders!" Bran roared, and the air turned electric.

"Ahrin, stay with Malachi." Maura's blade flashed as she drew it, her stance balanced, predatory. "Now!" she commanded, and the crew snapped to action.

The clash of swords erupted, sharp and relentless. The acrid tang of gunpowder burned in my nostrils as shots rang out, the crack of flintlocks echoing over the water.

Amid the chaos, a wide plank was lowered from our deck to theirs, a tenuous bridge between order and anarchy.

Men charged across, their faces contorted with fury, blades catching the pale sunlight as they met their foes.

My heart thundered as I gripped the railing, watching the dance of battle unfold before me. The sea churned below, indifferent to the violence above.

And yet, through the chaos, Maura stood resolute, her voice cutting through the tumult like a beacon. "Hold steady! They're testing our mettle—let's show them why Erius is a name to be feared!"

This was her element, the storm she seemed born to weather, and as the tide of battle surged, I couldn't take my eyes off her.

"She's remarkable, isn't she?" His voice carried a faint reverence, as if Maura were more than flesh and blood—some myth made real. "Even a princess isn't immune to her charm."

I said nothing, though the warmth rising to my cheeks betrayed me. Malachi noticed, his knowing chuckle rolling softly like a wave against the hull.

A question lodged itself in my chest, uncomfortable and insistent: had they been something once? But Maura's words to the privateer echoed sharply in my mind—"I much prefer women". No, Malachi wouldn't have stood a chance with her. But I would. The thought struck me like a sudden gust, stealing my breath, and my steps faltered.

The clash of steel on steel just ahead jolted me back to the present.

"Malachi!" Maura's voice rang out, sharp and commanding over the chaos above deck. She fought with a fluidity that was more like art than battle, each strike calculated and precise.

"On it, Captain!" he called back, extending a hand to me. "Care to see how quickly I can end this skirmish?"

I took his hand, and he led me swiftly below deck, past the chaos. The room we entered was unlike anything I had expected. Netted shelves lined the walls, stacked high with jars of unidentifiable substances—some translucent and glowing faintly, others dense with powders in unnatural hues. It was part laboratory, part apothecary, but entirely fascinating.

"I don't know what they are, not exactly," Malachi began, his voice carrying an almost boyish excitement as he held up a jar of something that shimmered like molten embers. "But I call them Thermalurkers. They haunt the hydrothermal vents deep beneath the waves, thriving in heat that would melt the flesh off any other creature. Bioluminescent thermophiles," he added, as if that explanation alone should suffice.

The jar in his hand caught the light, the liquid inside shifting between hues of molten orange and deep crimson, like a captured flame. Malachi's fingers brushed its surface with a kind of reverence, and I caught a faint gleam of pride in his expression, as though he'd plucked the substance from the depths of the sea with his own hands.

"They're more than just microorganisms," he continued, scanning the crowded shelves, his eyes narrowing in thought. "Their bodies hold heat, absorb it, and then.." He paused for dramatic effect, glancing at me with a grin. "Release it. Violently."

"What does any of this have to do with ending the skirmish?" I asked, my fingers drifted over the tops of nearby jars.

Without answering, he turned back to the shelves and retrieved another jar. This one was filled with a fine, pearly powder. "Do you know what this is?" he asked, holding it up for me to see.

"No," I admitted, my voice quieter now.

"Ground pyrophyllite," he said, as though the name alone should illuminate its purpose. He didn't wait for me to ask, pouring a measured amount of the powder into a smaller vial. The delicate substance fell in a graceful cascade, pale and glittering like powdered moonlight. Then, with careful precision, he added a small amount of the Thermalurker's luminous secretion to separate jar.

"We don't know why it happens," Malachi admitted, his tone lighter now, as if this mystery only added to his delight. "But when the Thermalurker's secretion meets the pyrophyllite, the reaction is... volatile." He paused, his gaze meeting mine with the weight of unspoken implication. "A rapid exothermic reaction, to be precise. Or, in simpler terms—an explosion."

"You're planning to use this... concoction on their ship?"

"Exactly." His tone was matter-of-fact, almost casual.

"But wouldn't cannons be easier?"

"They'd see a cannon attack coming, and they'd retaliate. We can't risk damage to our ship. It's far too important for our journey to—" He hesitated for a heartbeat, his jaw tightening as if he'd said too much. Then, with a faint smile, he added, "So I'll dive under their ship and set this mixture where it'll do the most damage."

"You've done this before?"

"Plenty of times." He flashed me a confident grin, his surety almost infectious.

He strode to the door but paused, turning back to me. "I could ask you to stay here, where it's safe. But I think you'd disagree with me."

"I'm not staying below deck," I said, folding my arms. "I'll be where the excitement is."

Where she is, I thought.

"Do you know how to use one of these?" There was a teasing lilt to his voice as he unsheathed his sword and offered it to me, hilt-first.

I nodded, though it was mostly a lie. My fencing lessons had been more about grace and form than actual combat. As my fingers closed around the hilt, the unfamiliar heft of the blade made my arm sag slightly. Still, I lifted it with determination, willing myself to seem capable.

"Good," Malachi said, his smile returning. "Stay starboard, then. All the action tends to congregate on the opposite and things are about to get interesting."

We ascended back to the deck, the air heavy with smoke and salt, the sharp clang of blades ringing through the chaos. The skirmish raged on, unrelenting, as Malachi moved toward the starboard side, lowering a rope ladder with steady hands.

"Be careful," I called softly, my voice barely audible over the din.

He glanced back, a faint smile curling his lips. "You too," he murmured, and then he was gone, descending into the watery embrace of the waves.

I turned back to the fray, my pulse quickening as my eyes caught on Claude, one of Erius' crewmen. He grappled with an enemy, his stance faltering, desperation etched into the lines of his face. Instinct took over, an unfamiliar yet undeniable surge of resolve propelling me forward. My grip tightened on the cutlass, its weight both foreign and empowering in my grasp.

With a single thrust, the blade pierced through the man's back. His body went rigid before collapsing in a lifeless heap at Claude's feet.

He turned to me, his expression one of stunned gratitude, though it mirrored the shock still coursing through me. "Thank you, Your Highness," he said, his voice tinged with awe before he disappeared back into the melee.

I stared down at the lifeless form before me. The man's unseeing eyes bore into nothing, a silent reminder of what I had done. The cutlass remained lodged in his body, an extension of my will—and of my survival.

I did that.

The thought should have unsettled me, yet shame and regret were nowhere to be found. In their place was something far more primal: the burning need to protect, to endure. And, if I were honest, a strange flicker of exhilaration.

Before I could dwell on the sensation, an arm snaked around my waist, pulling me into a firm hold. "There you are," Maura purred, her voice low and teasing, her breath warm against my ear.

Her mischievous smile sent a spark of something unnamed through me. "Brace yourself," she warned, her tone laced with anticipation.

The ship rocked violently beneath us, a tremor so sudden and forceful it stole the breath from my lungs. My gaze snapped to the other ship, its towering masts sinking lower and lower, as though dragged into the depths by an invisible hand.

"Malachi?" I whispered, my voice barely a breath, my wide eyes locking onto Maura's.

She gave a small nod, her expression brimming with quiet pride as her gaze lingered on the sinking vessel. "Set the sails, men!" she commanded, her voice cutting through the chaos like a blade. "Push any stragglers into the sea!"

Her grip on me loosened, though her hand lingered on my waist for a fleeting moment—a gesture that felt as steadying as it was reluctant—before she stepped away entirely.

"What about Mal—"

Before I could finish, his voice cut through the air. "Here! And alive!"

I spun toward the sound, relief blooming in my chest as I saw him, dripping wet, clinging to the railing. Two crewmen hauled him over, their hands steadying him as he stumbled onto the deck, grinning despite his soaked state.

"Fine work, lads! Once we make port in Cyanderis, the drinks are on me!" Maura's laughter rang above the fading clamor of the battle as she slid her blade into its sheath. She strode toward Malachi, clapping his shoulder with a firm squeeze that spoke volumes more than words ever could. Approval. Pride. Gratitude.

Her words took a moment to settle in my ears, but when they did, my feet moved of their own accord, quickly catching up to her. My hand found her forearm, fingers curling around the worn leather of her bracer.

"Cyanderis?" I asked, my voice softer than I intended, but sharp enough to betray my disappointment. "We're returning to Cyanderis?"

She turned to me, her lips quirking into that signature smirk of hers—the one that never failed to make my chest tighten. "After tomorrow night, I'm to return you there. That was the deal, remember?"

"I haven't made my decision yet." My voice trembled on the edge of defiance, but I steadied it.

"We're setting course regardless," she replied, her tone softening as her smirk melted into something more tender. "Just in case your decision leans that way." Her brow furrowed slightly, a faint crease forming between her eyes, and her gaze drifted across my face.

Her hand rose, slow and deliberate, her thumb grazing the curve of my cheek. The gesture sent a shiver spiraling through me. "You have blood on your face," she murmured, her voice low, almost chiding. "Were you hurt?"

My hand flew to my cheek, fingers brushing against the tacky remnants of blood. Not mine. The memory of the pirate I had felled flickered in my mind, vivid and unyielding. I swallowed hard. "It's not mine," I said softly. "I'm fine."

"Let's get you cleaned up," she said, her voice dipping into a whisper that lingered in the air like an unshed promise. She turned and began walking toward the captain's quarters, and without hesitation, I followed.

I leaned against the desk, the cool wood pressing into my palms as I watched her move with quiet purpose. She retrieved a small bowl and a jug of water. The soft pour of water into the bowl filled the space between us, and for a moment, it was the only sound.

She soaked a cloth, wringing it gently before stepping toward me. The silence stretched taut, unspoken questions lingering in the air. I didn't know how to break it—didn't know how to voice the storm of indecision raging within me.

Cyanderis. The weight of its name alone felt heavy on my tongue. If I returned, I would return to duty, to a life of obligation that rippled far beyond myself. But here—here was freedom. The sea had been my dream, and she had given it to me. Yet dreams had consequences, and mine was not just my own to bear.

The damp cloth brushed my cheek, cool and tender against my skin. Her hand steadied my face, her touch both gentle and commanding. Maura's focus was unwavering, her brows knit slightly as she dabbed away the remnants of blood.

She traced the corner of my lips, pausing as though caught in thought.

"Did it get on my lip?" I asked softly, my voice barely above a whisper. The thought of someone else's blood so close to being ingested churned my stomach, but her touch eased the discomfort.

"Just a little," she murmured, her voice low, almost absent. She brought the cloth to my mouth, but instead of its coarse weave, I felt the warmth of her thumb brushing over my lower lip. Slowly. Deliberately.

Her gaze lingered, heavy and intent. I watched the subtle bloom of warmth spread across her features. Her thumb traced my lip again, slower this time, and my breath hitched as my lips parted instinctively.

"Did you... get it?"

"...Yeah," she said, but her hand lingered a moment longer before retreating, the spell between us crumbling.

"Maura." Her name left my lips like a prayer, quiet yet desperate, a plea I could no longer hold back.

"Yeah?" she said, her voice gentle, almost cautious. She placed the cloth in the bowl, but her eyes flicked back to mine, curiosity and something else—something unspoken—dancing in their depths. Perhaps it was the same unspoken thing that resided within me.

I reached for her, my fingers brushing her cheek as I turned her face toward me. *Now or never,* I thought, as the weight of indecision dissolved beneath the pull of this moment.

My hand slid into her hair, fingers tangling in the silken strands as I drew her closer. My eyes fluttered shut as I guided her lips to mine, the world narrowing to the point of contact.

She froze for a heartbeat, and in that breathless pause, I feared I had been mistaken. But then she leaned into me, her lips pressing against mine with a fervor that matched the racing of my heart. One kiss melted into another, the barrier between us crumbling as her hands found my hips, lifting me effortlessly onto the desk.

"You've gotten better," she murmured against my lips, her voice rough with affection and mirth.

"I had a good practice partner," I replied, breathless, as her lips trailed a line of fire down my neck.

Her hand slid beneath the fabric of my dress, her touch firm yet cautious as it traced the curve of my thigh. Each kiss she pressed to my collarbone was unhurried, deliberate, leaving warmth to linger on my skin like the sun's final rays before dusk. There was a tension building within me, an ache I had no words for, a gravity drawing me closer to her even as I struggled to steady my breath.

"Are you certain this is what you want?" Her voice was soft, almost reverent, though her gaze was anything but hesitant. When I glanced down, I saw her eyes fixed on mine, searching. It was then I realized how tightly I clung to her—one hand buried in her hair, the other gripping her shoulder as if she were the only thing anchoring me in this storm.

"I am," I stammered, though the unsteadiness as my voice betrayed me. "I just—"

I stepped down from the desk, closing the distance between us until our bodies met. She held still, her presence grounding me as I took a deep, shuddering breath.

"Can we... can we go at my pace?" My voice was barely above a whisper, each word laced with hesitation.

"Of course," she murmured, her thumb grazing my cheek. "Tell me what you want, and I'll do it."

I nodded, though the words still faltered on my tongue. "Could you... lie on the bed?"

She obliged without question, stepping back toward the bed. Before she could lower herself, I reached out, tugging at her coat and hat. They slipped from her shoulders, discarded onto the floor with carelessness. I took her hand, guiding her to sit, then gently pressing her down until she reclined.

Gathering the hem of my dress in both hands, I bunched the fabric at my thighs, clambering onto the bed to straddle her. Her hands came to rest on the outside of my legs.

I leaned forward, pressing my lips to hers with a boldness that felt foreign yet instinctive. My hands traced upward, cupping the curve of her chest through her blouse. The soft gasp that escaped her lips was like a spark catching kindling, igniting a fire within me. This felt so similar to my dream, that I worried one wrong move would awaken me.

When her tongue swept against mine, I welcomed it eagerly, matching her rhythm with a growing confidence. My hands moved of their own accord, tugging at the fabric until it parted, my fingers brushing bare skin and gliding over her nipple. Her breath hitched, and for a moment, her lips stilled against mine.

Panic gripped me. *Had I gone too far? Did I do something wrong?*

I froze, withdrawing my touch as I pulled back.

Maura looked up at me, her hair splayed across the pillow like strands of dark silk. In that moment, she looked almost otherworldly—a goddess given form, a dream I was afraid to wake from.

"What's wrong?" she asked, her brows drawing together in gentle confusion.

"I... I don't know what I'm doing." My confession came out in a rush, heat blooming across my cheeks.

She smiled then, a soft, knowing smile that eased the knot in my chest. "That's all right," she said, her voice warm and steady. She leaned up to kiss me again, her lips brushing mine with infinite patience. "There's no right or wrong here, Ahrin. We go at your pace. This is about what you want."

"But I don't know what I want."

I wanted her—her touch, her approval, her presence—but the specifics eluded me. All I knew was the rush of my pulse and the ache that refused to be named.

"That's okay too," she said, her tone never faltering. Her hands slid up to my hips, her touch light but steady. She took one of my hands, guiding it to rest on my inner thigh. "Show me," she whispered. "Show me what makes you feel good."

One might assume such a task would be straightforward—a simple act of self-awareness. Surely, one knows their own body better than any other. Yet, no lessons had been granted to me on the art of pleasure, not beyond the stilted whispers of the court's matrons or the hushed, clinical instructions on how to endure one's wedding night. For those daring enough to lay hands on erotic novels, there were glimpses—half-instructions hidden within the florid prose of those pages. I had tried, fumbling and uncertain, to mimic what I'd read. Alone, it was one thing. But here, under her gaze, it was another entirely.

My breath wavered as I willed my fingers to move, slipping beneath the lace of my undergarments. There, my fingertips met a warmth and slickness I hadn't been fully aware of before. My body, it seemed, had known the path before my mind had caught up.

Tentatively, I let my fingers glide, exploring with slow deliberation. I sought out that delicate place where sensation coiled tightly, that familiar bundle of nerves that sent tremors through my limbs. My lips parted, a shuddered exhale escaping as pleasure unfurled within me.

When I dared to look at her, I found Maura watching. Her gaze was fixed on me, unwavering, her hazel eyes heavy with something hungry. Her lips parted slightly, her breathing shallow. One hand cupped her breast, her fingers splayed as she teased the dusky bud of her nipple, rolling and pulling it with a careful slowness. The sight of her—so unguarded, so consumed—all because of me, sent a thrill through me.

I am doing well. She is enjoying this too. The thought emboldened me.

My fingers dipped lower, tracing the edges of that entrance I had only dared explore in solitude. I hesitated a moment, then pressed forward, one finger easing into the slick heat. A moan slipped past my lips, unbidden, as my body clenched and yielded in equal measure.

I kept her gaze, unwavering, as my fingers pressed deeper, slow and deliberate, drawing soft whimpers from my lips. My free hand trembled as it reached for the folds of my dress, gathering the fabric in a bundle and pulling it higher, baring more of myself to her. It was a gesture that felt both vulnerable and bold, my heart thrumming like the beat of a distant war drum.

Her eyes drank me in, the weight of her desire wrapping around me like a velvet shroud. That look—it was a wildfire, devouring hesitation and filling me with a need that went beyond reason. I didn't want it to dim, didn't want that fire in her gaze to waver.

No, I wanted more.

I wanted her attention, her focus, her yearning to grow until it consumed us both. With every movement of my hand, every soft sound that escaped me, I offered more of myself to her, silently pleading for her to take what I couldn't yet voice aloud.

Her voice broke through the haze, low and rough like the rumble of distant thunder. "Can I feel?" she asked, as if she could read the dirty desires that plagued me.

"Please," I breathed.

She reached beneath me, her movements slow and deliberate. Her fingertips brushed against mine, her touch soft as silk. She didn't intrude but traced the motion of my hand, feeling through the damp fabric of my undergarments. Her touch, even through that thin barrier, sent jolts of heat coursing through me, heightening every sensation.

"Are you near the edge, or shall I guide you there?"

Her voice, low and unsteady, was more a caress than a question. Each word seemed to press against my skin, an intimate touch that left me breathless. For a moment, I could not answer, lost as I was in the storm she had stirred within me.

But then her gaze found mine, and I knew I didn't need to speak. She could see it—the fragile quiver of my lips, the unsteady rise and fall of my chest, the longing written into every trembling inch of me.

Her fingers slipped underneath the damp lace, brushing against my own. Together, we moved as one, her touch guiding mine with an intimacy that stole the breath from my lungs. The quiet, rhythmic sound of our union filled the cabin, mingling with my shallow breaths. I fought to hold her gaze, but the building pressure inside me forced my head to tip back, my lips parting in a wordless plea.

My strength faltered, and my hand fell away, leaving her to take over. She moved with a knowing precision, her thumb circling that delicate, aching place that sent waves of pleasure coursing through me. Her fingers curled just so, pressing against a spot I had never discovered, one that sent me hurtling toward a bliss I had never imagined.

I couldn't think, couldn't speak—only feel. My thighs quivered against her, and my hands found the bed, fingers curling into the fabric. My body tensed, suspended in that exquisite moment just before the fall.

"Come for me, princess," she murmured, her voice a velvet caress as her lips brushed over the swell of my breast.

Her words unraveled me. "M-Maura," I cried, her name tumbling from my lips. My body arched, every muscle tightening as the sensation crested and broke, leaving me adrift in its wake. My fingers clenched the sheets as I rode the waves, grinding against her hand as though she alone could anchor me.

For a time, the world was still. Her fingers slowed, though she did not pull away, grounding me with her touch. Our gazes locked, and in her eyes, I saw more than desire. I saw devotion, a depth of feeling that left my heart pounding anew.

A flutter of laughter escaped me, breathless and unsteady. "Can we do it again?" The question felt almost childlike, a shy yet eager request that left my cheeks burning.

Maura smiled, that slow, disarming curve of her lips that made my heart stutter. She pressed a kiss to my chest, her lips lingering over the sensitive peak that slipped out of my bodice.

She looked up at me, her voice a low promise. "As you wish," and I knew she would give me the stars if I only asked.

Chapter Six

Anchored in Devotion

The wood beneath my boots groaned with every step, the sound echoing softly against the mid-morning air. A breeze carried the salt of the sea to me, though it did little to distract from the restlessness coiling within my chest. My eyes roamed the deck in search of her, drawn by an ache I could scarcely name.

I had awoken to the lingering warmth of her absence, the bed still soft where her body had lain. The imprint of her lingered everywhere—on the rumpled sheets, in the faint scent of her on my skin, in the vivid memories still branded into my mind. I told myself she must have gone to attend to her duties, yet I couldn't banish the quiet yearning that had stirred me from the comfort of the cabin.

"*I want to stay,*" I had said, my voice trembling with conviction. The memory unfurled itself as if summoned: Maura's face, haloed in the young golden light of dawn, her breath warm against my thigh, her lips tracing my skin. "*Promise me.*" she had murmured, her words heavy with hope, with longing.

And I had answered her in kind, my voice as unsteady as the waves that rocked the ship beneath us. "*I promise. I will remain by your side forever.*"

The heat of that moment crept back to me unbidden, pooling in my cheeks and racing down my neck. I pressed my hands to my face, as if to quell the blush blooming there. Was it folly to make such declarations in the throes of passion? Or perhaps it was then, when truth was stripped bare and we were both laid open, that my heart had spoken its most honest words.

Unable to remain idle any longer, my feet carried me below deck, the dim corridor lit only by sparse lanterns swaying gently with the ship's movements. I sought her still, though now my path had direction. One of the crew had mentioned a meeting today—Bran, Malachi, and Maura. The captain's quarters had been otherwise occupied—the remnants of our passion and my sleeping form—and they had gathered instead in Malachi's laboratory.

My steps faltered as I approached the closed door, my back finding the cool grain of the wooden wall. I hesitated, the muffled cadence of their voices seeping through the cracks, their tones measured, their words indistinct.

Before I could decide whether to linger or move on, a warm weight brushed against my legs. Mr. Wiggles, with his sleek fur and ever-curious eyes, demanded attention. I crouched, my fingers threading through his soft coat, finding the spot beneath his chin that drew a gentle purr and sway.

But Mr. Wiggles seemed to have no time for extra affection today. With an unrelenting determination, he padded toward the door, nudging it open just enough to slip through, leaving it ajar.

"Wiggles," I whispered, my voice barely carrying. I reached for him, but he was already gone, his tail disappearing into the shadows of the room.

The door, left open a crack, betrayed the voices within.

"We'll be nearing their shores by dusk," Malachi's voice carried, steady and low, weighted with purpose. "This is sooner than we planned."

"It's fine," Maura said, her tone calm but firm. "Ahrin has said she wants to stay aboard with us."

Bran's reply was a sigh laced with irritation. "We should have retrieved it when we captured her."

"Does she know?" Malachi asked. "The real reason we need to return to Zostera again?"

A silence fell, heavy as a tide before the storm.

"No," Maura said at last.

"Then how do we know she'll help?"

There was another pause, and when Maura spoke again, her voice was softer but no less resolute. "I know her better than anyone. She will—Mr. Wiggles..." Her tone shifted, her words trailing off as they softened further. "Sneaking in again, are you?"

Footsteps sounded, drawing closer. My heart leapt to my throat.

I stepped back quickly, smoothing my breath and adjusting my pace to something casual, as if I had just been approaching.

The door swung open, and there she was—Maura, her hands cradling the indignant little magpie cat. She set him down outside the threshold, her sharp eyes meeting mine. "Ahrin," she greeted, her voice slightly elevated, a flicker of surprise in her expression. "Good morning. I meant to return before you woke, but—" she glanced back into the room briefly—"we can finish this discussion later. Stay the course," she called over her shoulder.

"I wasn't awake long," I replied softly, the words automatic, my mind still tangled in the snatches of conversation I had overheard.

Her lips brushed against mine, silencing any further response. Her fingers wove through my own, and her steps guided me gently, purposefully, back toward the deck.

I offered her a smile, one I hoped seemed easy, but beneath it, my thoughts churned like a storm-tossed sea.

Three days. A number spoken as though inconsequential, yet now it pressed upon me with weight. Was it mere coincidence, or was there a reason she needed to return to Zostera so urgently? What else had they been after when they came for me?

My gaze swept from the horizon to the deck, my thoughts as restless as the waves. How could I bring this up? How could I speak my unease aloud without it unraveling us?

"Why are we still sailing toward Cyanderis?" I asked finally, my voice breaking the uneasy quiet between us. "I can tell we're heading closer and closer to Zostara's shores." My words wavered; I had no map, no understanding of our exact position, but I hoped she wouldn't notice that.

At first, Maura didn't reply. Her lips parted, then pressed into a thin line, her teeth catching briefly at her bottom lip. I recognized that look. It was the same one she wore when we were children, caught out in a lie she couldn't quite shape.

My hand slipped from hers, the warmth of her palm suddenly too much. If she couldn't be honest, I would force her hand. "You didn't come to Zostara just for me, did you? There's something else you're after. Something that's drawn us back toward those shores, even when you weren't sure I'd stay."

My voice carried more bite than I'd intended, but I couldn't take it back.

"Ahrin..." Her voice softened as her gaze flickered to the deckhands nearby, their glances darting in our direction. "Can we discuss this in private?"

"So it's true?"

"I didn't say that."

"But you didn't deny it."

The silence stretched, taut and heavy as a drawn bowstring.

"Maura, I'm your..." I faltered, the word catching on my tongue. What were we? Lovers? Friends? Something that refused to be so easily named? "We are friends," I settled, though the words felt small. "Friends don't keep each other in the dark. Please, just tell me the truth."

Something flickered across her face, a crack in her usual composure. Her brows knitted, and her gaze hardened briefly, though not unkindly. "You're right," she said at last. "Come. Let us talk."

Maura led me to the captain's quarters, the door closing firmly behind us. She gestured for me to sit, pulling out a chair by the desk, and I obeyed, though my nerves prickled. From a drawer, she withdrew a leather-bound journal, its edges frayed with age. She placed it on the desk, her hand lingering briefly on the cover before stepping back. "Open it," she said, her tone neutral, though her gaze remained fixed on me.

I did as she bade. Inside, charcoal sketches greeted me—creatures of land and sea rendered in sharp, precise detail. Some I recognized from the tales whispered in court, others were unfamiliar, monstrous. The drawings were paired with scrawled notes, a hunter's observations, a scholar's study. I turned the pages slowly, my curiosity mounting, until I reached one marked by a scrap of cloth.

Here, the sketches became specific—sirens. Their half-human, half-fish forms etched in painstaking detail. My breath caught as I took it in.

"Do you remember," Maura began, her voice low, "how I told you Captain Roberto came to Florwyn five years ago?"

"Yes," I said slowly, glancing up. "You said he was looking for something."

"He was looking for the owner of this journal...because of this." She turned the page and tapped it with her finger.

The drawings now showed a map—or rather, a fragment of one. A jagged wall of rocks was sketched in the center, encircled by swirling waters. It was the Dead Sea.

"We were close to it once. That specific spot. When we ventured into the Dead Sea. These sketches—they were showing us the way."

Turning the page, my fingers traced the next drawing, the lines forming the image of a sunken palace glittering with impossible treasures. I recognized it, though I didn't want to believe. "Wait...is this what I think it is?"

"Maristell," she whispered, the name a dagger of cold down my spine.

It had always been a legend whispered among sailors, a tale too wild for reason yet too enticing to ignore. Beyond the Perpelagust Sea, it was said, lay the Dead Sea—a realm treacherous and cruel, a domain seemingly ruled by vengeful gods. Its tides pulled with an eerie will of their own, and its sirens sang songs crafted to ensnare the unwary.

But for the rare sailor bold—or desperate—enough to brave its waters and reach its heart, the prize was said to be beyond imagining: Maristell, the fabled underwater island of the sea gods. It was a place where treasures from every corner of the oceans were drawn, hoarded by divine hands. Gold, jewels, relics—every gleaming prize awaited, nestled among the gods' own riches. And for the one who dared claim it, the promise of fortune unending.

"But...Maristell isn't real."

"But it is." She sighed, leaning on the desk. "Captain Roberto and his crew, myself among them, followed this journal. It led us to the heart of the Dead Sea, but there, we found a wall—a jagged, circular barrier of rock. The water around it was unnatural, pulling us toward it like a living thing. And the sirens..." Her voice trailed off, her gaze distant. "They were everywhere, guarding the wall. Maristell lies beyond it, but we couldn't find a way through. This journal...he made it through. Abraham, the man who wrote this, he saw it. He sketched it.

But he lost his mind," Maura said grimly. "When Captain Roberto found him, he was raving in a tavern, drawing and redrawing the same images. People called him mad, but Roberto thought he could decipher the sketches, follow his trail. He was wrong."

Her tone darkened as she reached into another drawer and pulled out a pile of worn sketches, laying them before me. "A little over a year ago, we set sail for Maristell. We came so close, but we were still missing something. That missing piece cost us most of the crew—and Captain Roberto."

My chest tightened.

"A few months ago," she continued, "we heard a rumor. Someone who knew Abraham before he fell into madness claimed he left more of his notes in Zostara, hidden in

Florwyn's naval base. That's why we're heading there. To finish what we started."

Her words settled heavily between us, the weight of them undeniable. The secrets, the risk, the yearning—it all clicked into place. This was more than an adventure; it was a quest, one steeped in danger and ambition.

Maristell was real. And so was the pull it held over Maura, just as it did for Captain Roberto.

Some of her words lingered, clinging to my thoughts like seaweed tangled in a net. "A few months ago," she'd said. The phrase gnawed at me.

"You could have come for me sooner?" My voice cracked, disbelief threading through my tone.

"It's not that simple, Ahrin."

"How is it not simple? You've been captain for over a year, Maura. You didn't come for me until the very last moment—until the hour when breaking your promise was all but certain."

Her expression tightened, her voice steadying as though she were anchoring herself against my rising storm. "My captain was like a father to me. When he died, I was grieving—we all were. Half the crew was gone, the ship in ruin, and I had to rebuild from nothing. I had to keep us afloat." She paused, hands gripping the armrests of my chair with a white-knuckled desperation as she turned it to face her, the scrape of wood against the floor like a distant thunderclap.

"I have loved you since we were children, Ahrin." Her voice softened, cracking in its vulnerability. Slowly, she lowered herself to her knees, her hands coming to rest at my waist as she looked up at me with a rawness that stole my breath. "It hurt—being away from you, not knowing if you were safe, if you were happy. But I had one chance, one sliver of opportunity to infiltrate Zostara without being noticed, and I used it to get you. Not the notes, not Maristell. *You.* The promise I made to you mattered more than anything. Even if I couldn't make it in time, and you were in Thalassia, by his side. I would have come for you regardless."

"You... love me?" My voice faltered as my hand rose, almost without thought, to cup her face.

"Yes," she said, her eyes glistening as she leaned into my touch. Her hand covered mine, holding it against her cheek as if afraid I might take it away. "More than the salt in the air, the sound of the waves, or the pull of the tide. I have always loved you."

"So... we're more than friends, then?"

A faint smile curved her lips, teasing yet tender. "I would never take the time to learn every curve of your body, to map every place that makes you melt, and to commit every sound of your pleasure to memory if we were just friends, Ahrin."

Her words sent heat rushing to my cheeks, a warmth that spread through me like the tide cresting over sun-warmed sands. She lifted my hand to her lips, pressing a soft kiss to my palm as her gaze caught mine.

"Do you have any more questions?" she asked, her voice a low murmur. "Or will you let me show you just how devoted I am to not being 'just friends'?"

"Please," I breathed, the single word barely escaping my lips.

Maura's hands slipped beneath the fabric of my gown with a reverence that had my body melting with anticipation. Her touch was a whisper against my skin, her fingers trailing slow, deliberate lines along my calves before moving upward, tracing the tender curves of my thighs. As her palms reached my thighs, she paused—only a breath—before coaxing my hips upward, lifting me. The chair's sturdy frame caught me as I melted into its embrace, my gown now a silken tide pooled at my waist. Without thought, without shame, I parted my thighs, inviting her closer.

"It's not a throne," she murmured, her voice low and edged with desire, "but this chair is mine. And it's only fitting that a princess be bowed to and worshipped on it."

My breath caught as her lips brushed against the sensitive skin of my inner thigh, her words igniting a heat that spread through me like wildfire. "I thought," I managed, my voice trembling with anticipation, "pirates didn't bend for the crown."

Maura glanced up at me through her dark lashes, her lips ghosting over my undergarments. "A captain can make an exception," she purred, her fingers sliding beneath the delicate fabric shielding me from her. With a slow, deliberate motion, she drew it aside, baring me to her.

Her mouth descended, and the first press of her lips against me was like a spark to kindling, setting every nerve alight. Her kiss was soft yet commanding, a promise of the devotion she intended to show. She worked her way closer, her tongue tracing gentle, exploratory strokes before pressing deeper, tasting me with a hunger that sent my head falling back against the chair.

She moved with unhurried precision, her lips parting as her tongue delved into me, each stroke a revelation that left me trembling.

Her hands gripped my thighs, steadying me as I arched toward her, the ache within me growing with each flick and swirl of her tongue. The wet heat of her mouth was overwhelming, her movements orchestrated with the skill of someone who had learned every secret my body held.

Her nose brushed against the sensitive peak of my clit, a teasing pressure that made my breath hitch and my fingers tangled in her hair. I held her to me, my hips lifting, chasing the pleasure she offered so willingly. She hummed softly, the vibration sending another wave of sensation coursing through me.

Every kiss, every movement of her tongue was deliberate, a symphony of devotion that built and built until I thought I might shatter from the intensity of it. The slickness between my thighs grew, her name spilling from my lips in gasped prayers as she brought me closer to the edge.

And when I fell—when the pleasure crashed over me like a tempest—I clung to her, her mouth grounding me as I trembled and broke apart against her lips. Her kisses softened, her touch turning tender as she guided me back to myself.

When I finally found my voice, it was little more than a whisper. "You've shown your devotion... Captain,"

Maura looked up at me, her lips glistening but curved lazily in satisfaction. "A pirate knows how to cherish the most precious treasures," she said, her tone soft but laced with teasing warmth. "And I always take care of what's mine."

She stood, and an unspoken pull between us guided my body to hers. I pressed her back against the desk, my hands finding purchase on either side of her, caging her in. I wanted her to feel it—the depth of my devotion, the heat of my desire. I wanted her to know she was as much mine as I was hers.

No words passed between us as I pressed further, my lips claiming hers in a kiss that tasted of salt and sweetness, the lingering trace of myself still on her tongue. My hand wandered, slipping down the front of her trousers. When my fingers found her, warm and slick, I felt her smile curve faintly against my lips—a moment of playful surrender.

I traced the edges of her desire, teasing softly, searching for the place that would unravel her. When her breath hitched sharply, I knew I had found it. Her hands gripped the desk as she leaned back, offering herself to me without restraint.

My lips left hers, traveling a slow, deliberate path down the column of her neck. I kissed her there, the delicate skin soft beneath my mouth, tasting the faint salt of her. My tongue followed the curve of her throat, down to the swell of her breasts, where I pulled her shirt aside, freeing her to my touch.

I cupped the fullness of her breast in one hand, holding her steady as my tongue circled the peak, teasing her sensitive nipple. The soft pants that escaped her lips spurred me on, and I took her into my mouth, sucking gently, then firmer, as her body arched into me.

My fingers delved deeper, slipping inside her warmth, hooking gently in a rhythm that mirrored the pounding of my own heartbeat. She moaned for me, her voice a melody I wanted to hear again and again. Her hips began to grind against my hand, seeking more, and I gave it to her—pressing further, moving faster.

Her head tipped back, the smooth line of her neck exposed as her breath quickened into soft, broken cries. My mouth returned to her breast, tongue flicking over the hardened peak as my hand worked her closer to the edge. Her body tensed, a sharp gasp spilling from her lips as the crescendo hit. She shuddered, her release blooming beneath my touch, leaving her trembling and undone.

As her breathing slowed, I steadied her with one arm, our foreheads resting together in a tender moment of quiet connection. Her eyes fluttered open and she gave me a kiss—gentle, loving, unhurried.

"I love you," I breathed, the words slipping free as naturally as the tide.

I think I have always loved you—a truth long buried, now stirring from the depths of my mind like a forgotten melody rising to the surface.

Chapter Seven

Through Tempest and Song

"Reminds you of the good old days, doesn't it?" Maura's voice drifted over my shoulder.

"Yes..." I murmured, glancing at her with the faintest curve of my lips. "But I'd rather not relive the times we were caught red-handed. So hush, if you please."

Her quiet chuckle followed me as we crept along the shadowed outskirts of Florwyn's naval base, our steps muffled by the damp earth.

After our *'conversation'* yesterday, Maura had confided in me that my remark to Malachi—about sneaking into naval bases to procure maps—had sparked his interest. It was his idea that she ask my help. Though I'd never set foot in Florwyn's base before tonight, I had studied maps of the town's defenses, its strongholds. Curiosity had been my guide then; now, necessity took its place.

"There should be a tree northeast of the southern gate," I whispered, my eyes scanning the outline of the towering portcullis ahead. "It will look... different from the others."

"This one's certainly... different," Maura said, her fingers brushing over the bark of a massive oak nearby.

The tree stood like a sentinel, unnervingly perfect. Its trunk bore no scars of time—no burrowed holes from insects, no jagged marks from storms. Its branches swayed gently in the breeze, too graceful to belong to nature.

As I approached, I kept my gaze fixed on it, the stories of illusions playing tricks on the mind lingering at the edge of my thoughts. To look away was to risk losing its form, or worse, the passage it concealed.

My hands moved over the smooth bark, searching for a telltale sign. The moment my fingers brushed a softer notch in the wood, I pressed. A faint click echoed, followed by a series of mechanical whirs. A panel slid open, revealing a narrow, dark passage hidden within the tree.

"So, this is the work of Cyanderis' Divine Treasure?" Maura asked, her brow arched as she peered into the opening.

"Partly," I replied, stepping closer. "But the illusion? That's a witch's handiwork."

I led the way inside, my palms brushing against cold stone as we descended a spiral of narrow steps. The passage sealed behind us with a low rumble, leaving us cloaked in darkness.

Every continent held a Divine Treasure, a powerful relic that bent the natural world to the will of its keepers. A gift from the gods themselves. It was said that only the ruling council could lay hands on it, their authority safeguarded by its ancient magic.

"If I remember correctly," I whispered, my voice barely rising above the sound of our steps, "this corridor ends at a fork. The paths lead to the old servant's tunnels from when the base was a noble's estate."

My fingers outstretched, brushing against rough stone until I felt the corridor come to an end. Two doors flanked me, each cold beneath my touch. "This one," I said softly, opening the door to our left.

Faint slivers of light filtered through the cracks in the stone walls, guiding us into a narrow passage. The air here was thick with silence, heavy with the weight of secrets long buried.

"So, we are in Zostera." Maura's voice was soft, her words breaking the fragile silence.

"I know,"

"I know the pressures that weigh on you," she continued, her steps slowing as her gaze flicked to the stones beneath her feet. "I've always known. I just..." Her teeth caught her bottom lip, her hesitation hanging between us like a thread ready to snap.

I paused, turning back to her. "What is it you're trying to say?"

She inhaled deeply, the sound of it filling the narrow corridor. "I don't want you to regret leaving all of this for me. If you can't come back to the ship, if you choose to stay... I won't hold it against you."

Her words twisted something inside me, the quiet ache of doubt trying to take root. But I wouldn't let it.

"Maura," I said gently, reaching for her hand. My fingers wrapped around hers, and I pulled her forward, guiding her down another shadowed hallway. "It's not just for you. I want to leave for me." My voice dropped lower, more resolute. "Zostera will endure without me. Eventually, I'll let them know I'm alive and well. But I refuse to carry the weight of their expectations any longer—not for a crown, not for duty."

I let the words sit between us, my thoughts spilling forward. "I know they'll be disappointed that I won't fulfill the path set before me. Marrying into another kingdom to secure resources will fall to one of my brothers now. It's selfish of me, I know. But sometimes, being selfish is the only way to breathe."

Now that I had a taste of this. Of the freedoms and pleasures the sea had offered me, I could not go back. For I knew if I did, I would be a cloud of regret and longing that loomed over those around me. Jasper and I did not deserve such a fate.

Her hand tightened in mine, and I glanced at her briefly, her features painted with shadows and stolen light. She said nothing, but the unspoken understanding in her gaze was enough.

"I believe this is it," I said at last, my steps faltering as we reached a hidden doorway. The faint glint of a metal ring caught the light, the outline of the wooden frame barely visible beneath the subtle glow of the passage.

I pressed my ear against the wood, the cool surface grounding me as I strained to hear beyond it. Silence greeted me, deep and unbroken. My fingers found the ring, slipping around it as I pulled slowly, the faint creak of the hinges breaking the stillness.

"There are usually guards posted outside chambers like this," I whispered, glancing back at her. My finger rose to my lips in a shushing gesture. "Once we step inside, no words."

The door eased open, revealing the archive room. Shelves of scrolls and weathered documents lined the walls. Long tables stood in the center, their surfaces scattered with parchment, wax seals, and quills. A handful of torches burned low in their sconces, casting shadows across the room. The air was thick with the scent of old paper and melted wax.

I stepped inside, casting my gaze over the sprawling archive. Everything was organized with a logic I could only begin to grasp. Some scrolls labeled by location, others by cartographer or scribe. The chance of finding a section dedicated to the fabled Maristell seemed slimmer than catching moonlight in my hands, but the possibility compelled me forward.

Maura moved quietly beside me, her fingers brushing against the edges of documents as she searched by name, Abraham's surname eluded us.

My heart thrummed in time with the distant shuffle of guards outside the door, each faint creak of their boots sending a chill along my spine. I turned to the unlabeled maps, my fingers lingering over worn scroll casings. My fingers drawn to a dark leather casing. And there inside it was a map bearing the distinct charcoal strokes I had seen in the journal. My breath hitched as I unfurled it, revealing not only a map of the continents but intricate sketches of the Dead Sea, more sketches of the sirens with haunting eyes, and then of Maristell itself.

I motioned Maura closer. Her shadow fell across the parchments as she leaned in.

The sketches sprawled before us—a palace deep below the sea's depths, gilded halls overflowing with treasures. Notes scrawled in a hurried hand circled key points, detailing siren songs and the currents of the Dead Sea.

"There's so much gold there, so much wealth..." Maura's voice dropped to a reverent whisper. "You could buy Zostera a future without Thalassia."

The map of the Dead Sea stretched wide before me, its jagged borders and swirling currents drawn with a detail that felt almost alive. My gaze lingered over the intricate sketches, my fingers tracing the charcoal lines as if they held some hidden truth within their smudged edges. However, it was the second map, tucked beneath it like a forgotten whisper, that caught my breath.

Unfurling it, I revealed a tapestry of stars and moons, their celestial dance intertwined with meticulous coordinates. I spread it beside the larger map, my fingers moving instinctively to trace the numbers, to match the markers. The lines led me to a spot on the encircling wall of the Dead Sea. And then I saw it: a sequence of eclipses, past and future, their dates carefully etched.

My heart quickened.

"When sun and shadow cross as one, the waves reveal their mark."

The words spilled from my lips, soft as a nursery rhyme, and when I lifted my gaze, Maura was already looking at me. The realization passed between us like a spark, igniting the weight of the myth into undeniable truth. The path would only open during an eclipse.

A distant clatter of keys shattered the fragile silence, followed by muffled voices outside the door.

We moved as one, gathering the maps and sketches with shaking hands, rolling them into their leather casing. The door groaned faintly as we slid it open and slipped back into the darkened service tunnels, the stone walls closing in around us.

"I swear I heard something," a voice muttered, low and tense.

"I didn't hear a thing, and there's no one here," came the reply, followed by the retreating echo of boots.

In the quiet, Maura began to murmur under her breath, her voice carrying the cadence of an old song, the rhythm of a tale as old as the sea itself:

"Beyond the Perpelagust's tide,
Where tempests weave their spell,
The Dead Sea waits with secrets deep,

And whispers of Maristell.

The sirens sing their haunting tune,
To lure the sailor's pride,
Their voices sweet, a cruel deceit,
Where only fools confide.

When sun and shadow cross as one,
The waves reveal their mark,
A fleeting sign, a thread of time,
To guide the bold through dark.

But dare you tread where legends warn,
And tempests rise to swell?
For none return who seek to learn
The truth of Maristell."

Her words wrapped around us like a spell, the haunting rhythm of the ballad filling the silence as we navigated the narrow corridors. At last, she stopped, her gaze heavy with meaning.

"The eclipse will show the way through," she said quietly. "The next one is in seven days, Ahrin. If we leave now, we can make it." She paused, her fingers brushing mine. "But... last chance to stay in Zostera. It's going to be dangerous, and—"

I silenced her with a kiss, my hand cupping her face as my lips pressed against hers. When I pulled back, I met her gaze, steady and unyielding. "I promised I would stay at your side," I said softly. "And *we* always keep our promises."

The first sign was the sky—a gray veil that swallowed the horizon and bled the vibrancy from the world. It was as though we had sailed into a dream untethered from the waking realm, where the air held its breath and time seemed to falter. A thin mist curled across the deck, clinging to the timbers like a whispered warning, while the sun disappeared behind a thick curtain of cloud, leaving only its dim suggestion behind.

"Welcome to the Dead Sea, Your Highness," Bran said, his hands steady on the helm, his voice as calm as if he hadn't just guided us into the maw of a legend. Ahead, jagged outcroppings of rock loomed like the bones of a forgotten beast, their edges sharp enough to slice the sky.

I drifted toward the railing, the salt-laden air cool against my face, and peered down into the waters below. Black as spilled ink, the sea refused to yield its depths, reflecting only a fractured distortion of the clouds above. I felt it then, the unshakable sense of being watched, as though the sea itself carried a mind and will of its own.

Time unraveled here; minutes stretched into hours, hours collapsed into moments. Only the rising moon, creeping slowly to veil the sun, broke the monotony of the gray. As its shadow deepened, Maura gave her command, her voice sharp with purpose.

"Lower both anchors. The current is too cunning for just one."

She leaned close, her presence a tether against the unease curling through my chest. Her hand guided the spyglass to my eye, tilting it eastward, beyond the ship's bow.

"Do you see it?" she murmured, her breath warm against my ear.

But I saw nothing—only darkness painted in shades of crimson as the moon eclipsed the sun. The waters glowed faintly, the light like blood spilled across their surface.

"Just beyond, the tide begins to pull," she said, her voice low, almost reverent. "And there—the barrier."

Malachi approached, the warm flicker of his lantern cutting through the gloom. He unrolled a map and spread it across the railing. "Follow the path eastward," he instructed, his finger tracing a narrow line that curved toward the suspected break in the barrier. "Take the dinghy, and it'll guide you straight to the opening."

"The dinghy?" I asked, my brow arching as I turned to Maura.

Malachi's gaze flicked between us, his lips twitching into something like exasperation. "You didn't tell her the plan?"

"I..." Maura hesitated, her composure slipping. "I wasn't going to involve her. I meant to go alone."

"You can't," I said sharply, my voice cutting through her excuse. "What about the crew? What about me?"

Maura sighed, her shoulders sagging under the weight of her defiance. "There are reasons," she said, her voice quieter now. "Reasons why you and the crew cannot follow me."

I stared at her, confusion knitting my brow. "What reasons?"

Her gaze met mine, steady and unflinching. "Do you know the origin of the sirens, Ahrin?"

"No," I said, wary of the sudden shift.

"They were women once," she began. "Women stolen from the land, taken by force, defiled, and drowned. Their rage consumed them, and the gods—merciful or cruel, I do not know—gave them purpose instead of peace. Their songs call to the greed of men, luring them to their deaths."

Malachi added, his voice grim, "We only escaped the last time because of Maura. The sirens' magic doesn't work on women. She saved us."

My stomach turned, a hollow ache settling in its place.

"We're safe here, on the edge of their waters," Malachi said, gesturing toward the expanse beyond. "But once you cross that threshold, everything there will work to drown you. Their songs, their illusions, even the sea itself."

"And why can't I go?" I demanded, anger flaring in my chest.

Maura stepped closer, her hand brushing my cheek, her eyes brimming with something far deeper than fear. "Because I couldn't bear it if you didn't return," she whispered. "This is a quest for foolish pirates, not—"

"Not a princess?" I interrupted, bitterness sharpening my words.

"No," she said firmly. "It's not for the love of my life."

The weight of her words settled between us, an ache too heavy to speak of. I swallowed hard, then laced my fingers with hers.

"There's no point to this freedom if I cannot share it with you," I said, my voice trembling with conviction. "I'm coming with you."

Her eyes searched mine, and for a moment, I thought she might refuse. But then she nodded, her resolve softening as she turned to Malachi.

"Prepare supplies for two," she said, her voice steady now.

And just like that, we became conspirators against fate, bound together by love and the promise of a legend.

Malachi returned with a burlap sack and placed it with care on the deck. The soft thud broke the tension, though his expression remained solemn. One by one, he began to pull items from the bag, each a curious item of ingenuity and necessity.

"You're already familiar with these," he said, holding up a glass jar of Thermalurker's secretion, and another of powdered pyrophyllite. Then he reached deeper, retrieving something I hadn't seen before—a vial filled with a blue paste. "This," he began, his voice steady, "is for the waters. If the tales of Maristell's depths hold true, it will help you withstand the cold below. It's an algae that reacts to the chemicals in humans. It is safe."

I nodded, my gaze flickering to the next item. Two slender ropes entangled around small, rounded glass jars. Within each floated tiny jellyfish, their translucent forms glowing with a soft, ethereal purple light.

"Tie these around your waists," he said, placing them in my hands. "Their glow will guide you if you're brave—or unfortunate—enough to enter the dark waters."

The weight of his words settled on me, pressing against my chest. "We'll have to," I murmured, my voice distant as my gaze wandered to the endless expanse of black water stretching beyond the ship. "If we mean to retrieve anything at all."

"Speaking of, the more you haul, the heavier your dinghy will become. The added weight shall anchor you against the tides, making it harder for the sea to tip you or sway you off course on your journey back."

Maura chuckled softly, a sound that cut through the unease. "Now you're just trying to tempt us to strip the sea bare," she said, her tone light, though her eyes lingered on him with an unspoken gratitude.

Before I could respond, she stepped away, her boots echoing against the deck as she approached Bran at the helm. I watched as she plucked her hat from her head, placing it atop his with a teasing smile. Whatever she whispered to him was lost in the murmur of waves and the rustle of the wind, their quiet camaraderie a brief reprieve from the weight of the moment.

Malachi's voice brought me back, his words measured as he finished explaining the remaining contents of the sack—simple tools, mundane yet vital. When he finally handed it to me, his hand lingered briefly against mine.

"You two can do this," he said, his voice a quiet conviction. "We all have faith in you."

Soon, we were seated in the dinghy, the ship looming behind us like a sentinel against the encroaching night. A single lantern hung from a short wooden post, casting its golden glow across our small space.

The water stirred as the dinghy dipped into the waves, the gentle splash of its descent sending ripples into the abyss. Maura handed me an oar, and together, we rowed forward, each pull of the water a slow, deliberate rhythm.

It wasn't long before I noticed it—the strange motion of the sea, as though it held a will of its own. The stories had whispered of this, of waters that defied nature, pulling and twisting, leading sailors deeper into their grasp. It wasn't a current in the way I'd known it. This was something alive, something deliberate.

Maura's hand moved steadily as she withdrew a compass, its needle trembling yet resolute. "Keep straight," she said, her voice calm but firm. "No matter how it pulls, no matter what you feel. Keep it steady, and it'll lead us to the opening."

Her words settled over us like a commandment, and I found myself clinging to them. Each stroke of the oar felt heavier now, the water seeming to resist us and yet beckon us all at once. As we moved forward, silence claimed us—save for the creak of the oars and the quiet murmur of Maura's breath beside me. The pull of the Dead Sea grew stronger, its grip tightening, and yet we pressed on, steady and unyielding, drawn toward the heart.

The hairs on my arms rose before the sound even reached me—a warning from my body, instincts older than thought. The melody that followed was haunting, a song too beautiful for this world. It wound through the air like a siren's whisper, slipping beneath my skin and wrapping around my ribs. Every instinct screamed for me to turn back, to flee, but the sound held me captive.

I swallowed hard, my throat dry despite the mist hanging heavy in the air. As we drew closer to the wall of jagged stone, the song became clearer, more defined. It was a woman's voice—or perhaps many voices—woven together into a single, aching hymn. It was no language I knew, yet it was unmistakably the language of the sea: ancient, boundless, and cruel.

Sirens.

My breath hitched as I saw them, their pale forms perched on the outcroppings like specters. The eerie light bathed their ghostly white skin, turning it faintly red, as if they had been dipped in blood.

"Maura," I whispered, her name barely escaping my lips.

"They can't entrance you," she said sharply, though her voice trembled with urgency. "The song will try to fill you with fear. Don't let it. Don't focus on them. Focus on going forward."

But I couldn't. My gaze locked onto their terrible beauty, and I drank in every detail with a mix of horror and awe. Their sleek, powerful bodies—an amalgamation of sea and woman—shimmered like a predator's beneath the eclipse's light. Their sharp features—inhuman yet eerily familiar—seemed carved from the sea itself. Their lips parted, but they did not move as the song flowed effortlessly, as though the music poured straight from their throats.

The sound sank into my chest, blooming into something I didn't recognize until it consumed me. This was not fear, it was sorrow.

A tear slipped down my cheek, and I brought a hand to my heart, pressing against the ache that had taken root there. *What is happening to me?* The grief was overwhelming, a crushing weight that felt like loss—of what, I couldn't say.

"Ahrin!" Maura's voice cut through the haze like a blade, jolting me. My oar sat uselessly upon my lap, and I realized I had stopped rowing. The dinghy had veered off course, its bow tilting dangerously toward the wall of jagged stone.

The sea roared around us, its waves clawing at the boat. Rain began to fall, sharp and stinging against my skin, and the wind whipped my hair into my eyes. I blinked hard, gripping the oar and forcing myself to row, every stroke a desperate struggle against the water pulling us toward the rocks.

"We're too far off course!" Maura shouted, her voice barely audible over the storm and the unrelenting song. Her eyes darted to the wall of stone, then back to me. "We have to correct it!"

Before I could answer, the world tilted. A wave surged beneath us, and the boat pitched violently. I reached for Maura, but the movement came too fast.

And then I was consumed.

The cold hit me like a blade, slicing through my clothes and skin as I plunged into the water. The sound of the sirens' song was muffled now, replaced by the deafening roar of the sea.

Chapter Eight

Descending New Depths

For a moment, there was nothing but darkness—a void so absolute it pressed against my chest, crushing the air from my lungs. The tide was relentless, dragging me further into its merciless embrace. My arms clawed against the water, muscles trembling as I fought to rise, to break free of the suffocating depths.

But the sea had other plans.

The current surged, thrusting me downward as a figure sliced through the shadows above. It descended with eerie grace, its form glowing faintly in the murky expanse. Half woman, half fish—a siren, her beauty cold and unearthly, a thing of nightmares spun in silver and darkness.

I froze, my mind at war with instinct. *Should I swim deeper, risk the abyss, or fight my way to the surface?* My heart drummed erratically as I kicked upward, the lightless water pressing against me like a living thing. She was close now, her movements liquid, effortless. My breath burned in my chest, my vision fraying at the edges.

And then she was there.

Her arms wrapped around me, colder than the sea, colder than death itself. I wanted to thrash, to scream, but her touch was firm, unyielding. Her webbed fingers cradled my jaw, tilting my face toward hers. Her pale lips parted, and in a moment too surreal to comprehend, she pressed them to mine.

A rush of icy air filled my lungs. Breath where there should have been none. She released me, her luminous eyes inscrutable as she drifted back into the shadows, a specter dissolving into the depths.

For a heartbeat, I hung there, suspended in the void. Then a flicker caught my eye—purple light, faint and pulsing, like the jellyfish that hung in the jars tied to our waists.

Maura.

I kicked with renewed purpose, my muscles screaming as I propelled myself toward the glow. I shouted her name, though the water swallowed the sound, muffling it into nothingness. The surface broke above me, the light fractured and distant, but I pushed harder, desperate.

At last, I breached.

The air tore into my lungs, raw and stinging, as I gasped her name again. "Maura!"

Her head snapped toward me, her voice ringing out, frantic and sharp. "Ahrin!"

We swam toward each other, the waves thrashing between us. Her hands found my face, trembling but steady as she pushed the hair back from my cheeks.

"Are you all right?" Her voice cracked, her breath coming fast.

"I'm sorry," I choked out, my lip quivering despite my best efforts. "I'm so sorry."

Her arms wrapped around me, anchoring me against the sea and the fear still coursing through my veins. "It's okay," she murmured, her voice soft against my ear. "It's okay."

"One of them kissed me," I murmured as I stared into Maura's steady gaze.

Her lips quirked into a faint smile, though her fingers rose to rub at the space between her brows. "Me too," she admitted softly. "It let me breathe beneath the water... I think they saved us."

The notion hung in the air. *Saved us.* Would it have been the same if we were men? Their song, ancient as the sea itself, was meant to tempt, to lure, to destroy. And yet, for me, it worked differently. For Maura, it had seemed to pass her by entirely, leaving her unbothered by the treacherous beauty. Then they granted us air instead of stealing it. Why had they spared us?

Maura dipped her head below the surface, her hair a dark cascade that glimmered in the crimson hue of the eclipse. When she rose again, water trickled from her jaw. "I can still breathe underwater," she said. "Let's hope this gift doesn't expire anytime soon."

"What do we do now?" I asked, swallowing the knot of unease that had settled in my throat.

Her eyes turned toward the horizon. "That's where the tide is pulling us," she said, nodding toward the unseen force tugging at our bodies. "We let it take us to Maristell."

The words hit me like a shiver down my spine, a mingling of hope and dread. I wanted to argue, to ask what if Maristell wasn't real? What if this pull led only to a sailor's grave? But there was no strength left for doubt. We were out of options. So I chose to believe. To believe in the stories, in her unyielding faith in the sea.

We clung to each other as the tide claimed us, the rain stitching itself into the rhythm of the waves. The eclipse painted the waters with a ghostly red, the world around us cast in a mariner's nightmare.

As we neared the center of the Dead Sea, the pull growing stronger, I turned to Maura, one arm wrapped tightly around her waist. My hand found her cheek, saltwater beading on her skin. "I love you," I whispered, and before she could reply, I pressed my lips to hers, tasting the sea between us.

"I love you," she breathed as we parted, her words peace among the chaos. She kissed me again, her hands tangling in my hair, holding me as if she feared the tide might take me from her grasp.

And then, with one shared breath, we were submerged.

The pull became a torrent, dragging us down into the abyss. The world turned to black as the water swallowed the light of the eclipse, and only the faint glow of the jellyfish jars tied to us offered a glimmer of hope.

The current slowed, not to stillness but to something eerily gentle, like a hand guiding us instead of tearing us apart. The darkness began to bleed with light—purple, blue, pink, and green hues shimmering like starlight beyond the vortex of water encasing us.

Fragments of the dinghy swirled around us, reduced to splinters by the sea's rage, yet here, amidst the glow, it felt almost beautiful. A strange, haunting beauty, like the final verses of a song before the silence.

I reached out instinctively, my hand going to touch the watery wall of our descent, but Maura caught my wrist, her brow furrowed in warning. Her silent reprimand made me smile despite it all. Even here, she remained the compass that kept me steady.

Without warning, the current shifted again, and we were flung from its grasp, as if fired from a cannon. I hit a flat surface with a muted thud, sand and silt billowing around me as I arched in pain.

"Maura." Her name tore from me in a soundless gasp, my eyes frantically scanning the water.

And then I froze.

This was the floor of the Dead Sea, the fabled resting place of myths. This was Maristell.

Around me, bioluminescent fish and plants swayed, their light painting the seabed in shades of wonder. Jellyfish pulsed lazily in radiant hues, their tendrils like threads of spun moonlight. Scattered across the sand were treasures untold—jewels, coins, fragments of gold and silver glinting in the ethereal glow. And in the distance, rising like a dream from the sea's embrace, was the center of Maristell.

It's palace loomed, not of stone or brick but of coral and shell, its spires twisting like the bones of the sea itself. It was both delicate and immense, a structure alive with the pulse of the ocean, shimmering with colors too vibrant for the surface world.

Maura's hand slipped into mine, her grip firm, grounding me in this impossible reality. I turned to her, and she gestured toward the palace, her eyes gleaming with determination.

Together, we swam forward, hand in hand, toward the myth we had dared to chase.

There were no doors, no windows—only arches carved into the coral that mimicked the grandeur of human design. They rose in curves and spires that might have graced a cathedral on land, though here, they were softened by centuries of salt and shadow. We swam through, and as we passed beneath one such arch, a school of fish scattered around us, their scales brushing our skin like whispers.

Inside, the palace opened into chambers vast and strange, crafted from coral, jagged rock, and gleaming minerals unlike anything I had seen before. The walls shimmered with hues that seemed to pulse faintly in time with the rhythm of the sea. Pearls the size of fists nestled in open clams. There was wealth here and immeasurable beauty.

We swam further, ascending through tiers of chambers and hallways, the formations becoming reminiscent of floors and staircases. When we reached a grand staircase carved of pale marble, I faltered. It looked impossibly pristine, utterly incongruous amidst the coral and stone. My fingers brushed Maura's wrist, and when she turned, I pointed upward.

The top of the staircase shimmered as though we were ascending toward the ocean's surface, though logic told me it was impossible. We were too deep. No palace, no matter how immense, could pierce the surface from these depths.

Maura met my gaze, her lips parting in wonder, but she said nothing. Together, we swam up the staircase, the light above growing brighter. When we broke through, the sensation was jarring—air on our skin, cool and sharp. Both of us gasped, filling our lungs with oxygen as we pulled ourselves free of the water.

"I think it's an air pocket," Maura murmured, climbing the stairs further, her steps careful on the marble. She extended a hand toward me, her palm open and waiting.

I followed, my fingers tracing the smooth, damp railing as we ascended. The further we moved from the water, the more the space transformed. The coral and sea-rock faded, replaced by walls and floors that would have been at home in any palace on the continent. Marble mosaics gleamed under the faint reflection of light from below, while arched ceilings bore intricate carvings of waves and sea creatures.

"It's as though the ocean claimed part of the palace," I said, my voice hushed. "And yet this part... it remains untouched." Reminiscent to the sirens, this palace was like them. Both worlds colliding, neither entirely one nor the other.

She brushed her fingers against the wall, her expression distant. "Abraham's sketches couldn't have prepared me for this. Maristell is real."

I laughed lightly, though it carried a trace of concern. "The way you're speaking makes me think you didn't truly believe before we set out."

"I believed," she said, her gaze scanning the space around us. "I knew in my heart it was real. I just didn't expect... this." Her voice softened, and she turned to face me, her expression solemn but warm. "I'm sorry that we're trapped here. But I'm not sorry that it's you I'm here with."

Her words settled over me, and I leaned against the railing beside her, gazing down at the glowing waters below. "Isn't this a sailor's dream, though? Isn't this our dream?" I asked, a faint smile tugging at my lips. "We're surrounded by the sea, by treasure. No obligations. The water is calm, warm even, and for now, there seems to be no danger."

Maura rested her chin in her hand, her smile slow and teasing as she glanced at me. "And yet... it's just another cage, isn't it? One palace traded for another."

I turned to her, my expression softening as I lifted my hand to touch her cheek. "There's one difference," I said quietly.

"Wherever you are, I am free. Whether it's a palace in Cyanderis, a palace beneath the sea, a jail cell, or a drifting ship—nothing can diminish the joy of being by your side." My voice faltered slightly as I continued, but I held her gaze. "You may call me the greatest treasure in all of Zostera, but Maura, you are the greatest treasure of the sea. And you are mine."

Her cheeks flushed faintly, her smile broadening as she shook her head. "You've been reading too many of those books, Ahrin," she said, though her tone was playful. She stepped closer, the distance between us dissolving, and cupped my face in her hands. Her lips pressed to mine, firm and sure. I returned it, my hands tangling in her wet hair as I pulled her closer.

My lips stilled against hers, the motion fading as a faint sound crept into my awareness. It was delicate, barely a whisper at first, but it pulled at something deep within me. My hands slipped to her shoulders, resting idly as Maura's lips grazed my neck.

"I don't think I could ever get used to you tasting like the sea though," she murmured, her lips hovering just above my collarbone, her tone laced with affection.

There it was again—that sound. This time, I caught its direction, a low hum that quivered on the edge of recognition. It wasn't just noise; it was a melody.

"Ahrin?" Maura's voice was soft but laced with concern. She straightened, pulling back to meet my gaze. "Are you all right?"

"You don't hear it?"

Her brows furrowed. "Hear what?"

I stepped away, drawn like a tide to the moon. The sound grew clearer as I moved, each note sharper and more insistent. It was the same ancient song that had called to me when the sirens' voices first pierced the waves. I didn't answer Maura's question, my focus narrowing as though any distraction might silence it.

"Ahrin," she called again, following close behind me, her voice steady. But I was beyond words, driven by a pull I couldn't explain.

The sound led me through the palace's labyrinthine halls. At last, I reached two massive gilded doors. They were carved with intricate depictions of the sea—whales breaching, mermaids diving, waves cresting in frozen splendor—all inlaid with veins of gold. Without hesitation, I pushed them open.

The room beyond was vast and empty. Two tall windows stretched from floor to ceiling, the ocean visible beyond in all its luminous clarity. The light filtering through the water danced on the walls in rippling colorful patterns.

"I swear it was coming from here," I murmured, my voice trailing into the stillness.

I stepped farther in, my gaze drifting upward. That's when I saw it—suspended high above me, bathed in soft light, was a trident. It was unlike anything I had ever seen, its craftsmanship so perfect it seemed otherworldly.

Without thinking, I raised my hand. As if summoned, the trident descended, gliding through the air with a grace that defied logic. My fingers closed around its shaft, and the song that had led me here fell silent.

The trident was cool to the touch, its surface smooth as polished stone. Its pale blue hue shimmered faintly, threaded with white streaks that mirrored sunlight reflecting off the sea. The prongs were made of sharp, gleaming pearls, and etched along the shaft were markings—an ancient script I should not have been able to read but understood instinctively.

It was the song of the deep.

"That's a Divine Treasure," Maura said, her voice reverent and low.

"That's not possible," I replied. "There are only four, and they're on the continents, kept in palaces..."

Her gaze didn't waver. "We're standing in an underwater palace in the Dead Sea, Ahrin. We found Maristell. Is it so hard to believe the sea has a Divine Treasure of its own?"

I swallowed, my father's words echoing in my mind. *"The Divine Treasures grant too much power for one person alone. Greed and ambition destroy those who wield them, which is why they are shared among councils."*

Perhaps that was why it had been hidden here, deep beneath the waves, far from the grasp of mortal ambition. A power to command the sea... such a thing was too great for one land, one throne. And yet, here it was in my hands.

"It chose you," Maura said softly, stepping closer. Her hand slipped over mine, steadying my grip on the trident.

I couldn't deny it. It had chosen me. The impossible journey that had brought us here, the sirens' song, the trials we had faced—it all led to this moment.

"You are the queen of the sea, Ahrin," Maura said, her voice brimming with quiet conviction. "You are our queen, to all who tread these waters."

It was the way the Divine Treasures worked. They chose the bloodlines that reigned and now it had chosen once more. Only a fool would deny the sea.

"Queen maybe," I turned to her, a wry smile tugging at my lips. "You're still my captain, though."

Her laughter was soft, her eyes shining with something unreadable as she stepped back.

I raised the trident, the ancient song spilling from my lips, unbidden and unrestrained. The waters beyond the windows stirred in answer, a ripple turning into much more under my command. For the first time, I felt the weight of the power in my hands—a thing ancient and untamed, but mine.

"Ready to return to your ship?" I asked, my gaze steady on hers.

Maura arched a brow, her grin playful. "Yes, your majesty."

Epilogue

"You know that doesn't count as steering the ship, don't you?" Maura called from the deck below, shading her eyes against the sun with one hand. Her tone carried that playful lilt I could never resist.

"Are we not heading in the right direction?" I replied, laughing softly.

In moments, she closed the distance between us and plucked the trident from my hand with ease, redirecting my arms back to the wheel as though I were a wayward child in need of correction.

"You're commanding the tide to pull us there," she murmured against my ear, the faintest hint of a smile in her voice. "That's not the same as steering, love." She pressed a kiss to my cheek, her lips lingering just long enough to make me sigh in protest.

"Hey!" I pouted as she carried the trident off toward our quarters, the sunlight catching on the delicate curve of her profile.

Left to my own devices, I resigned myself to the wheel, inhaling the scent of the open sea. The light breeze ruffled my hair, the horizon stretching endlessly before us, unmarred by storm clouds or distant sails. There was a silence to the ocean that felt sacred, broken only by the creak of wood and the occasional slap of waves against the hull.

My gaze wandered across the ship. Smaller than Erius' vessel, our ship was humble—cozy, even. There were no hidden compartments stuffed with stolen treasures, no labyrinthine storage for weapons meant for raids. Just simplicity. Just *us*.

Well, us and Mr. Wiggles.

I chuckled as the ship's cat brushed against my calf before curling up lazily at my bare feet. His affection, fleeting as ever, ended the moment Maura returned to my side. Her arms slid around my waist, pulling me gently against her as her chin found its familiar perch on my shoulder.

"Are you excited to go back to Zostera?" she asked, though her tone lacked any trace of excitement.

I tilted my head toward her, curious. "I take it you're not?"

Her sigh was quiet, a ripple in the stillness. "We were just there."

"That was eight months ago," I countered, laughing softly. "And that hardly counted as a proper visit."

Once we had returned to Erius' ship, the sea had yielded to my command, treasures breaking through the surface like a chorus rising to meet the sun. Gold and jewels spilled forth in shimmering heaps, enough to please the crew and to sever the binds of duty tethering Zostera to a marriage with Thalassia. It had been a triumph, but there had been no time to revel in it. Not truly.

"My parents were relieved to know I was alive," I said softly, the words catching on the breeze like fragments of an unfinished thought. "But there was no chance to process any of it—me, you, us." Maura said nothing, so I pressed on. "And we didn't even see your father. They miss us. I promised them we'd spend a month on land, and—"

"And we always keep our promises," she interrupted, her voice a quiet murmur. She leaned in, her lips brushing the curve of my neck, sending a warmth through me that chased away the chill of the salt-laden air. "Alright," she sighed, surrendering her fragile protest. "I won't complain anymore."

My hand drifted back, threading through her hair as I turned to capture her lips with mine. "It's time for us to meet the parents properly—as betrothed," I whispered, the word carrying both pride and weight. "And besides," I added with a grin, "I need more books."

Her lips curved into a slow, reluctant smile, the faintest laugh escaping her before she pressed another kiss to my lips, this one lingering. "As you wish," she whispered.

NOTE FROM THE AUTHOR

The Princess Bride has been my favorite movie since childhood—the romance, the adventure, the humor... and, of course, Westley. One day, after picking up a special edition of the book, inspiration struck, and the tale of Ahrin and Maura took shape.

Thank you so much for reading my story! I'd be truly grateful if you could take a moment to leave an honest review and rating on Goodreads, Amazon, or any other platform you prefer. Your feedback makes a world of difference for small authors like me. If you'd like to learn more about me, explore my other works, or check out upcoming projects, please visit https://elijahher.com.

Thank you again for your support!

OTHER WORKS BY ELIJAH HER

"Binds of the Forsaken"

An achillean novel about reincarnation and forbidden love. In a modern world, the story follows a fallen angel and his soulmate, a retired mafia prince.

"Stakes 9-5"

An achillean novella about a dystopian future where vampirism is a man-made cure for disease and aging. The story follows a group of vampire hunters tasked with stopping the release of a new compound—one that could create an unstoppable breed of vampires.

"Ascendance of the Forgotten Prince"

An achillean novel about survival and reclamation as a magically-forgotten prince endures enslavement, political intrigue, and forbidden passion to reclaim his birthright.

CHARACTERS OF HMC

Ahrin Caldwell (She/Her)
Age: 21
Sexual Orientation: Bisexual
Species: Human
Personality Type & Sign: INFJ, Pisces
Physical Descriptions: Dark Gray Eyes, Black Hair, 5'9"
Favorites: Herb-roasted vegetables, honeyed pastries, herbal tea, citrus water, reading and journaling

Maura Vandross (She/Her)
Age: 21
Sexual Orientation: Lesbian
Species: Human
Personality Type & Sign: ENTP, Sagittarius
Physical Descriptions: Hazel Eyes, Brown Hair, Neck Tattoo, Facial Scarring, 5'11"
Favorites: Spiced fish stew, roasted shellfish, rum, mead, swordplay and stargazing